"I don't want to take advantage of you."

"Then let me take advantage of you," Kelly whispered.

John stared, his confusion eclipsed only by the strong flare of desire in his eyes. He stopped stroking her wrist and the first needle of panic pricked her confidence.

She'd already told herself she wouldn't blame him for rejecting her. She was engaged to his boss. He had every right to put a stop to this recklessness.

He dropped her hand. Her heart nose-dived.

"Look, John, I'm—"

She had no chance to let him off the hook. His hand came up to cup her jaw and his mouth covered hers with such a fierce swiftness he literally stole her breath.

Dear Reader,

The forecast this spring is for SHOWERS! Not the gloomy, wet kind that brings May flowers, but the baby, bachelor and wedding kind that brings happiness and true love!

And you're invited to all three! This month Debbi Rawlins hosts a bridal shower—but which of the two men in her heroine's life will be the groom?

If you've missed the two previous SHOWERS books, you can order them by contacting Harlequin Reader Service at, in the U.S.: 3010 Walden Ave., P.O. Box 9042 Buffalo, NY 14269; or in Canada: P.O. Box 609, Fort Erie, Ont. L2A 5X3.

The confetti's falling at American Romance. Don't miss the fun!

Regards,

Debra Matteucci
Senior Editor & Editorial Coordinator
Harlequin Books
300 East 42nd Street
New York, NY 10017

The Bride To Be... or Not To Be?

DEBBI RAWLINS

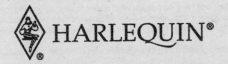 HARLEQUIN®

TORONTO • NEW YORK • LONDON
AMSTERDAM • PARIS • SYDNEY • HAMBURG
STOCKHOLM • ATHENS • TOKYO • MILAN • MADRID
PRAGUE • WARSAW • BUDAPEST • AUCKLAND

ISBN 0-373-16730-X

THE BRIDE TO BE...OR NOT TO BE?

Copyright © 1998 by Debbi Quattrone

This edition published by arrangement with Harlequin Books S.A.

® and TM are trademarks of the publisher. Trademarks indicated with ® are registered in the United States Patent and Trademark Office, the Canadian Trade Marks Office and in other countries.

Printed in U.S.A.

Chapter One

"Touch that and you die." Kelly St. James glared at her friend Ellie's hand as it hovered over the collection of miniature trolls Kelly had gotten for her eighth birthday.

Ellie sighed with disgust. "Maybe you should leave the room. You're missing the entire point of this exercise."

"Leave the room?" Kelly shuddered at the thought of letting her friend sort through her closets unchaperoned. She retrieved the sweatshirt Ellie had dropped into the Goodwill bag. "I don't want to do this anymore. It was a good idea for about two seconds."

Eyeing the sweatshirt, Ellie folded her arms across her chest. "Have you worn that since college?"

Kelly hugged the endangered fleece to her breasts. "Once."

"Once in eight years?" Shaking her head, Ellie held out a hand, a look of obstinate determination in her brown eyes. "According to the magazine article, this is precisely the kind of stuff you need to get rid of. Come on, Kelly, give it up. Unclutter your life."

Kelly reached for a hanger. Ellie could be stubborn

at times, but she was no match for Kelly. "Number one, it's my life. Number two, I'm moving into a bigger place. Why do I need to get rid of anything?"

"How is the house coming along, by the way? Will it be done before the wedding?" Ellie asked, and Kelly didn't fail to notice her friend's hand inching toward the trolls again.

"Gary says it should be, but I'm not so sure. The weather's been so cold this spring, they had to break ground late." She rehung the sweatshirt, then swept the trolls to safety, ignoring Ellie's pained look. "Have you ever dealt with contractors? They have to be the slowest, most unreliable bunch of guys this side of the Ozarks. I'm going to swing by this afternoon and see what's going on."

"Gary's in charge of the house construction," Ellie said, a wry smile tugging at the corners of her mouth. "You promised to stay out of it."

Heat bloomed in Kelly's cheeks, and she turned away from her friend. She really was trying to let her fiancé handle things. It had been nearly a month since she'd been to the house. She'd heard the snide remarks around town about her being the one to wear the pants in the family, and although she had no patience for such narrow-mindedness, she didn't want Gary to suffer the mean-spirited talk.

And he would. She knew him too well...since sixth grade when his parents had bought the neighboring farm. He'd never say anything, of course, but the remarks would sting. Just like they had in grade school when everyone thought he let Kelly push him around too much. Even then, he never challenged her. Sometimes, though not often, she wished he would.

"Gary is busy at work," she said, picking up the glass of lemonade she'd left on her dresser. "He can't stay on top of them like I can. He won't mind if I throw in my two cents."

"Two cents? There isn't enough gold in Fort Knox when you get involved in anything." Ellie pulled a brightly colored tie-dyed garment out of the closet and frowned at it. "I remember this skirt. It belongs to your mother." She raised her surprised gaze to Kelly. "What are you doing with it? I didn't think you were this sentimental."

Kelly quickly set down the lemonade and snatched the garment out of her friend's hand without meeting her eyes. "I'm not. Sunshine asked me to keep some of her things. That's another reason why you weeding out my junk isn't going to work. Her stuff is mixed in with mine."

A speculative gleam glittered in Ellie's eyes as she stared at the twenty-year-old skirt Kelly was balling up in her hands. "Why do you keep calling her Sunshine?" She finally asked. "She's asked you to start calling her Mom and everyone else calls her Susan now."

The doorbell rang and Kelly wasn't sure if she was relieved or irritated. She wasn't expecting anyone else, but she hadn't expected to get into a discussion about her wayward mother, either.

"That's Lana," Ellie said as she poked her nose into a bag of hair accessories sitting on the closet floor. "Want me to let her in?"

"Get out of my closet." Kelly narrowed her gaze. "What's Lana doing here? She's supposed to be baby-clothes shopping."

"Yeah." Ellie grinned. "But she didn't want to miss this."

"What do you mean by *this?*"

"You giving up an ounce of control. This will make Bachelor Falls history, you know."

"Very funny," Kelly said. When the doorbell sounded again, she slammed her closet door closed, making Ellie jump. "You get to tell Lana the party is over."

"No way. Now there's two of us to gang up on you," Ellie said over her shoulder.

"You've gotten awfully pushy since you became a married lady," Kelly grumbled while reopening the closet door and tucking her mother's skirt into the farthest, darkest corner. She heard Ellie's laughter echo down the hall, and couldn't help but smile. In the span of two short months, both her friends had married terrific men who made them glow with happiness. Hard to believe that in a matter of weeks she'd be joining their ranks. Well, maybe not the glowing part—but Kelly was far too practical to worry about that. Besides, she couldn't find anyone better or more stable than Gary.

Straightening, she dusted her hands as she glanced around her spare room. Clothes and decade-old magazines were piled on the bed and dresser. Two Halloween costumes were draped over the treadmill in the corner. It had been five years since she'd worn the Marilyn Monroe one, and at least seven since she'd squeezed into the Catwoman getup.

She sighed. Any sane person would dump this junk instead of moving it. She didn't understand why she was having so much trouble parting with the stuff.

Although maybe she didn't need to, since the new house would have four bedrooms and a basement....

"If I hadn't seen it with my own eyes, I would never have believed you were such a pack rat."

She turned at the sound of Lana's stunned voice, just in time to see her dump an armful of boxes onto the bed before resting her hands on her very pregnant belly.

"You've already stopped in my bathroom?" Kelly asked, appalled, as she watched Lana sort through the expired boxes of hair-color rinses, each containing a varying shade of blond.

Ellie stood peering over Lana's shoulder, her arms crossed, her head shaking. "Mind-boggling, isn't it?" She frowned up at Kelly. "I'm glad you're not blond anymore. I like your natural reddish brown color better."

Kelly reflexively touched her hair. She'd actually been thinking about going blond again for the wedding. Maybe she'd ask Gary what he thought. Although she doubted he had an opinion.

"You can throw out only the expired ones," she said.

Her two friends grinned at each other. Ellie promptly produced a large paper grocery sack she'd been hiding behind her back, and Lana swept the hill of boxes into the bag.

"How old are those magazines over there?" Lana asked.

"*Gourmet* and *Bon Appetit* are ageless. Don't touch them."

"Really?" Ellie tried to look impressed, but they'd been accomplices since they were old enough to talk and Kelly knew better than to underestimate that innocent lift of her friend's brows. "So, when was the last time you made one of the recipes?"

Kelly glared in response. Why had she allowed herself to get talked into this? At the time they'd read the article on spring cleaning, it had sounded like a good idea. If you're a pack rat, if you have a problem parting with your useless treasures, let your best friend glean through your closets for you, the article had said. She'll objectively know what you need and what to throw out.

Well, Kelly had changed her mind. She didn't want to part with her useless treasures. Instead, she wanted the author of the article shot.

She was about to order her two sidekicks out of the house when the look of genuine shock on Lana's face gave Kelly pause. Slowly she swept a gaze around the room, seeing it as Lana did.

A Shirley Temple doll sat atop two leaning stacks of Nancy Drew books. Today the doll might have been worth a lot of money, except that the hair had been whacked off in a fit of childish rage almost two decades ago. Kelly had long ago outgrown those displays of temper, but it had been too late to save her doll...her only doll.

She took a deep breath. She didn't need these trappings anymore. Did she? She had enough possessions and money and privacy and all the other things she'd grown up without. She supposed some psychologist would tell her this urge to horde was a form of rebellion against her childhood spent in the commune. But she didn't want to examine her behavior right now. She just wanted...she wanted change.

Her shoulders sagged. Which meant getting rid of the past.

"Okay, listen up," she said, grabbing her purse and keys and brushing away the last of her misgivings. "I'm leaving, but these are the ground rules."

The way two disbelieving yet hopeful pairs of eyes met hers almost made her laugh. These women were truly great friends, always there when she needed them. It had been that way for as far back as she could remember.

But she still didn't want them to see the water-colors.

"You can go through the guest room closet, the hall closet and the balcony storage closet. But stay out of my bedroom."

They exchanged glances and nodded eagerly.

"Not even a peek."

"Not even a passing thought," Lana said, already distracted as she picked up a stack of magazines.

"And if you have a doubt about anything… *anything* at all, you don't throw it out." The words had barely left Kelly's mouth before Ellie took her by the shoulders and urged her toward the door.

"You're in good hands," her friend said, "now scram."

"I mean it about my bedroom." Kelly's gaze locked with Ellie's until her understanding nod brought the reassurance Kelly needed. Then she twisted around for a final look before Ellie pushed her out the door. The lock clicked behind her.

Kelly's hand tightened around her keys but she squashed the urge to rush back in. Instead she focused her thoughts on the house.

It was going to be a perfect house. Her marriage was going to be perfect. She would have perfect kids, and they would all be perfectly happy behind their white picket fence.

Gary.

Guilt swirled like a spring tornado within her. She'd almost forgotten about her fiancé...the eventual father of her children. Which was rather silly. They had known each other forever. He was almost like a brother to her.

The sudden thought sent a dull ache to her chest.

She had to stop thinking of him that way. He was going to be her husband in four weeks. And he'd make a damn good one. Perfect, in fact. He was kind and sensitive and, above all, stable.

So what if he didn't make her glow?

JOHN CAPPEL LAID DOWN his hammer and took a swig of coffee from his thermos. The weather was still cool in the mornings, but by the afternoon it would warm up. Everyone told him that was fairly normal for late May. He'd only been here for a month, but what he'd seen of the Ozarks, he liked.

He liked Gary Sizemore, too. The fellow who'd hired him to do the finishing work on the new house was a nice guy. A couple of times he'd even sprung for a twelve-pack of beer for the men after work. Too bad John had to tell him his house wouldn't be completed in time for his wedding.

Taking one last gulp of coffee, John glanced at his watch. He stretched out the crick in his neck, then picked up his hammer and a handful of nails, slipping them into his flannel shirt pocket. It had only been a year since he'd turned his carpentry hobby into a job, and although it made more sense to wear a work apron like a lot of the men did, he couldn't seem to get in the habit of doing that. Canvas or otherwise, the idea of wearing an apron chafed. His aversion probably had something to do with his childhood, but he wasn't into analysis these days. He didn't want to have to think at all. He just wanted peace and quiet and to kick back and enjoy life.

"Hey, Cap, look what just pulled up." Dusty Tucker pushed back the bill of his baseball cap and let out a low whistle. "I'd buy whatever she's selling."

John let his hammer complete the swing he'd just taken, then turned to his gawking assistant. Dusty was a good, dependable helper, but at twenty-one he often still acted like a kid. His mother had died when he was just a boy and sometimes her absence in Dusty's life showed in the untutored way he responded to women. Although John could relate to the younger man's loss, he knew better than to gawk.

"Close your mouth, kid. I don't think she'd appreciate you staring like that," John said with a none-too-subtle nudge. Satisfied he'd gotten Dusty's attention, he gazed off toward the grassy parking area to see what kind of woman had gotten Dusty so wound up.

Sunlight glistened off a mass of chestnut-colored hair, the rays sparking streaks of golden red fire. There was a lot of it, thick and glossy, hanging to her shoulders and dusting the snug white blouse she wore.

Although she was too far away to get a good look at her face, he knew he hadn't seen her in town before. He would have remembered. Not just because she looked pretty even from this distance, but also because she didn't look or dress like the other women around Bachelor Falls. Her pants were white and tight like her blouse, yet there was a glamorous sophistication about the way she was put together.

"Hey, you just told me not to do that." Dusty punctuated his irritation with a jab in John's ribs.

He straightened. *Damn kid.* "You didn't see my mouth hanging open, did you?"

"Almost," Dusty mumbled low enough that John could barely hear. Louder, he added, "Who is she?"

"How would I know? Go ask her."

Dusty shrugged. "Okay."

John grabbed him by the shirt before he took a second step. He forgot how literally the kid could take things. "Hold on, tiger, looks like we're going to find out."

She'd stopped to talk with a couple of the other men, who pointed her in John and Dusty's direction, although John couldn't figure out what she'd want with either of them. He figured she might be a Realtor or decorator. They didn't see many women out here, for good reason. This was still a construction site and not always safe for a tourist. He was mildly surprised the men had allowed her to enter. Then again, he had a feeling men didn't say no to this woman very often.

She took her time picking her way through the maze of wood and brick, pausing to inspect an arched doorway or slowing down to frown at a piece of molding. For a moment he lost sight of her when she disappeared into what would eventually be the kitchen. But the clicking of her heels on the cement floor alerted him to her approach right before she emerged from the shadow of a newly constructed wall and into a patch of sunlight streaming in from the living room window.

Her hair lit up again, the golden red streaks blazing with health and vitality. Her complexion was flawless, except for a small beauty mark on her cheekbone near her left eye. Too bad she wore so much makeup.

"Are you John Cappel?" she asked in a brisk, no-nonsense tone. When he nodded, her topaz gaze flickered over him, resting briefly on his dusty hands, but she didn't hesitate to extend one of hers.

Her grip was solid and firm, surprising him. He'd pegged her as one of those high-maintenance, glamorous types, yet her tone and handshake hinted otherwise.

"I'm Kelly St. James," she said, and he blinked, trying like the devil not to show further amazement.

Dusty snorted. "No sh—"

John shot him a warning look. His assistant wouldn't hesitate to react openly to the woman they'd heard so much about. Knowing Dusty, he'd probably tell her she didn't look anything like the wicked witch of the Ozarks.

"Now would be a good time to knock off for lunch," John told him, and when Dusty hesitated, John lifted one practiced brow for emphasis. Seventeen years apart in age, John often felt like a father to the kid, and over the past three years they'd somehow developed a silent form of communication. Dusty knew this was no time to argue.

As soon as the younger man ambled away, John

transferred his attention to the woman. "How can I help you, Ms. St. James?"

"Kelly will do fine," she said, her gaze leaving his to survey the bundles of decorative molding stacked nearby. She took a deep breath, and his attention drew to the fabric tightening across her breasts.

Swearing to himself, he forced his gaze to her face. He was as bad as Dusty. But he was only human, after all, and physically, she was just his type—not too muscular but soft and rounded like a woman was supposed to be.

But that's where it ended. She was engaged to his boss. Besides, he'd heard about her famous temper, and he didn't suffer shrews well. No matter how good they looked.

He laid down the hammer. "Okay, Kelly, what can I do for you?"

"You can tell me this house will be completed before the end of June."

"Why are you asking me this?"

"Shorty says you're the boss."

"Shorty?" He frowned over her shoulder at the men grouped together near the entrance of the house, who were staring back at them with rapt interest.

"Oh, I think he goes by George now." She shrugged, a brief smile touching her rose-tinted lips. "We used to call him Shorty in grade school."

"*Shorty's* mistaken. I'm not the boss."

At his too brusque tone, her brows drew together as her haughty gaze raked a path across his shoulders, down his well-worn jeans to his steel-toed boots. As her appraisal made the return trip, the haughtiness faded from her face and her startled eyes widened a fraction as they raised to meet his. "Oh."

John shifted uneasily at the flustered look on her face. *Bloody hell.* Had he left his fly undone?

She slid a look over her shoulder at the rest of the men and he used the opportunity to make a quick check. Everything felt okay.

He snatched his hand out of harm's way just as she turned back to him, her expression guarded. In a cool voice, she asked, "Well, then, who's in charge?"

He immediately understood where she got her reputation for being difficult and controlling. As businesslike as she'd been before, there was no mistaking her no-nonsense attitude now. Her chin lifted subtly, as did her eyebrows, her steady gaze making direct contact with his, demanding an answer.

John mentally shook his head. Gary Sizemore was in deep trouble. The poor guy was too nice and easygoing to stand a chance with this woman.

"Not me," he said. "I'm just one of the worker bees."

Her eyes narrowed with suspicion. "Who do you report to?"

"Gary Sizemore."

"You don't have a supervisor here on the site?"

"Nope." He stooped to pick up his hammer. Her gaze followed to the action with disapproval. She thought he was dismissing her. Which he supposed he was.

"What exactly do you do, Mr. Cappel?"

"The finishing work." He probably should tell her to call him John, he realized, but he figured the point was moot. They wouldn't be having any more contact. He reached into his pocket for a nail.

"Correct me if I'm wrong, but doesn't the finishing work come at the end of the job?"

He half smiled. He knew where this was leading. "Yeah."

"So, you would know how close to completion this is."

He let out a huff of air. What the hell. He'd save Gary the aggravation of having to tell her the bad news. "You're not going to be spending your wedding night here, if that's what you're thinking."

A subtle shade of rose seeped into her complexion. She took a deep breath, her breasts rising and falling against the straining white blouse. The blush annoyed her, judging by her disconcerted reaction to it and the way she tried to avert her face. Both the blush and her reaction surprised him.

"Why didn't you tell me that in the first place?" She straightened, adjusting her shoulders and blessedly loosening the fabric across her breasts.

It was John's turn to avert his face. It wasn't like him to stare, but he had to admit he was having trouble keeping his eyes off her. There was something inordinately appealing about the way she moved, how her shoulders shimmied slightly when she seemed uncomfortable, or the way she pursed her lips into a soft pout while she was thinking.

"Why are you ignoring me?" she asked, and John swung his gaze back in her direction, nearly choking on his thoughts.

Ignoring her? He cleared his throat. "Sorry."

She frowned. "If you'll give me a minute, I'm sure

we can straighten this out, and you can get back to—'' she waved a pink-tipped hand ''—pounding.''

Relaxing his arm, he let the hammer fall heavily to his side. ''Straighten what out?''

''The completion date.''

''You're disappointed. I understand. But it's not a matter of straightening anything out. We're behind schedule.''

''Then work faster.''

John laughed, and lined up another nail.

''I'm not kidding. We have a contract with you people.''

''Which takes inclement weather into account,'' he said without looking at her. He took a couple of swings with the hammer, and the pounding drowned out her response. But from the brief glimpse he got of her expression, he had a feeling he didn't want to hear what she had to say anyway.

Still, although she was clearly unhappy, she hadn't lost her temper as he'd expected her to do. He should have known better than to listen to idle talk. Maybe she wasn't such a shrew. A determined, independent woman intimidated some men, especially in a small, laid-back town like Bachelor Falls.

''Would you please put that hammer down?''

Her impatient voice cut through his thoughts and he slid her a wry look. ''Thought you wanted us to work faster.''

She tilted her head at a haughty angle, her eyes sparkling with banked irritation, which made the corners of his mouth twitch. Then she folded her arms across her chest, causing her blouse to pucker.

He snapped his attention back to lining up another nail and drew back the hammer.

She sighed loudly, just as he took another swing, and from his peripheral vision, he caught her doing that little shimmy thing she did.

The hammer slipped, missing the nail, and smashed against his thumb.

He let out a yell.

Chapter Two

Kelly jumped at the guttural word that split the air. Not because she was offended. She herself had used that word upon occasion. But it'd been unexpected.

"Are you okay?" she asked, peering at the hand John Cappel cradled to his chest. His broad, solid-looking chest.

"No, I'm not okay. I just pounded the hell out of my thumb." He glared at her for a moment as if it were her fault that he'd been so clumsy.

"Will you still be able to work?" she asked, craning her neck, trying to get a look at the damage.

He lowered his hand, away from her inspection, the silence stretching so taut between them that she abruptly raised her gaze to meet his accusing navy blue eyes.

"Well?" she said.

"Thanks for the sympathy."

"I did ask if you were okay, didn't I?"

He huffed out an agitated breath, leaned back against an unfinished wall and continued to examine his hand.

"A bruised thumb is hardly life threatening." Men

were babies. They thought they were dying over the least little thing. Coddling them only added to their overreaction.

He bowed his head over his hand, probing it, and purposely ignoring her.

"Do you want me to look at it?" she finally asked when his sullen silence had grown too long.

"Just stay where you are."

"Excuse me?" She reared back her head.

"This is a construction site. You shouldn't be here."

"Of course I should. I'm the owner. Unless you think a woman's place is in the kitchen...a finished kitchen."

His eyebrows raised a sheepish fraction before he scowled at this thumb again. "Well, if you hadn't been—"

"You're implying that this is my fault?" she asked, stepping closer.

His gaze darted up in alarm. Although he had to outweigh her by seventy pounds and was a good six inches taller, he looked scared to death. It wasn't exactly a new experience for Kelly. A lot of men were intimidated by her. But she sure didn't expect this one to be.

She breathed in a long disappointed breath and his gaze flickered toward her chest before quickly skittering away. Sheesh. She hoped she hadn't popped a snap or something, and glanced casually at the front closure of her blouse. Thankfully nothing was showing.

"Gary is supposed to stop by this afternoon. I'll discuss the completion of the house with him."

"Don't tell me," she said, disappointment now warring with irritation. "I was right. You don't deal with women."

He sent her an amused look. "Actually, they're my favorite gender," he said, then returned his attention to a hand-flexing exercise.

Kelly frowned. As much as she hated to admit it, this man unsettled her. Although she was helpless to explain why or how. He was different.

He wasn't from around here, either. That was for sure. She knew almost everyone from Bachelor Falls, if not personally, at least by sight. The dark tan he sported also told her he hadn't been here long.

And his accent was British, possibly Australian. Although slight, it was undeniable. Especially when he got excited...like when he'd banged his thumb.

Her frown deepened. He simply continued to ignore her. She'd been wrong about him being intimidated. Amused, maybe, but not intimidated.

"So how's the thumb?" she asked, deciding to blow off his last remark.

"Like you said, I'll live."

His brows furrowed, and for a moment he looked like a hurt little boy who had just been told he couldn't go to the circus. She bit back a grin. He hadn't forgiven her for not fussing over him.

"Long enough to talk about completing this job?" she asked.

"It'll be completed. Just not before the end of June."

"That simply isn't acceptable."

He shrugged, as if he didn't really give a damn about what she found satisfactory, and patted his breast pocket. Where a wedding ring may have once been, a band of paler skin circled his finger.

Kelly's gaze flew to his face. She didn't know this man at all, yet the idea that he was married, or had been, startled her. She didn't know why. She had no business thinking about him in personal terms. She wanted her house done. That's all.

He withdrew a nail from his pocket and pinched it between his thumb and forefinger as if testing his ability to hold it. The skin was already turning purple around his thumbnail and she realized that his injury might be worse than she'd thought.

"You ought to put some ice on that thumb," she said, squinting for a closer look.

He didn't say anything, and when she glanced up he was watching her. A smile lifted half his mouth and as attractive as she thought he was before, her stomach got a little fluttery at the way the expression made his eyes glitter. His sun-streaked hair fell lazily across one dark brow and he casually swept it back with a tanned hand.

"Careful. You almost sound like you care," he said before turning to realign the nail.

"I'm not heartless."

"This isn't a good time to distract me."

"How am I doing that?" she asked, her annoyance rising when he chuckled. She straightened. "You're the one being rude by working while I'm trying to discuss the house."

"Don't you ever give up?"

"Not by a long shot."

He lowered the nail and hammer. "Look, Gary

hired me. I think this conversation should be with him.''

Kelly frowned. He had a point. "Okay. I'm free all afternoon. What time is he supposed to meet you here?''

''You're coming back,'' he stated, and his disgust couldn't have been plainer.

She bristled. ''Have I really been that unreasonable, Mr. Cappel?''

''You've already jumped down my throat about the house, made me smash my thumb and accused me of being rude. So by all means, call me John.''

She was speechless. No one spoke to her this way. And certainly not in this acerbic tone. She stared as he turned away from her to return to his work, and she was even more appalled to find herself ogling his butt.

It was round and firm and very solid-looking, molded by well-washed denim.

She exhaled sharply. She never noticed men's butts. Ever.

''I'll be back,'' she said as she started to back away, ''and I will get some answers.''

John didn't bother to look at her. He merely leaned over and flipped on his portable radio, sending the sounds of soft rock bouncing off the bare wood walls.

If he heard Kelly's irritated growl, he didn't acknowledge it.

JOHN GLANCED AT HIS WATCH. If Gary Sizemore didn't show up within the next ten minutes, John was going to call it a day and head home to a warm shower and a cold bottle of beer.

Seven hours after slamming his thumb, it still throbbed occasionally, but that wasn't what bothered him. He shook his head. Who would have guessed Gary's fiancée looked like *that?*

He finished storing his tools in the metal box and surveyed the ground for any loose nails he might have overlooked. It was starting to get dark and the small flashlight he kept with him wasn't going to be much use in the next fifteen minutes. Not for working in the house anyway. With the walls up, most of the twilight was shut out and the electrician wasn't scheduled to come out for another week yet.

Satisfied that he'd left the site in reasonable order, he made his way down the hall toward the kitchen and out the back door.

As soon as he stepped outside he saw the red compact car and knew it was hers. The rest of the men had left a half hour ago, and besides his Jeep parked ten feet away, there were no other cars around. Obviously Gary hadn't shown up. He didn't blame the guy.

John half sighed, half groaned as he approached his Jeep, set down his toolbox and reached into his pocket for his keys. The red Ford Escort's tinted windows prevented him from getting a good look inside, not that he was trying especially hard. He figured if he ignored her, maybe she'd give up and go away.

No such luck. The slamming of a car door forced him to look up. She was still wearing the tight white blouse.

He let out a frustrated breath.

"Has Gary come by yet?" She picked her way over the gravel, the heels of her not-so-sensible shoes sinking into the soft, rain-soaked ground between the rocks.

"No." He didn't wait for her to reach him. Swinging open his door, he stored his tools in the narrow gap behind his seat and set his radio on the passenger side.

"I don't get it. He should have been here by now," she said. Catching his smile, she added, "What?"

"Did he know *you* were coming?"

Her eyes narrowed, their smoky topaz color a striking combination with her chestnut hair. "What's that supposed to mean?"

He shrugged. "Just wondering if he knew you'd be here."

She folded her arms across her nicely rounded chest and he had to look away. "He'll be here, all right."

John glanced at his watch. "It better be within five minutes, or I won't be."

"He'll show up. Surely you can wait."

"Nope."

Loosening her arms, she dropped them to her side. "At least give him fifteen minutes. There was a lot of traffic in town."

He laughed. "There's never a lot of traffic in Bachelor Falls."

Kelly frowned. "It's not *that* small."

Noting her defensive tone, he decided not to comment further. He reached into the pocket behind the passenger seat and withdrew a navy blue baseball cap that had seen better days. After sweeping the hair off his forehead, he tugged on the cap.

"You really aren't going to wait, are you?"

"I can't."

"You mean won't."

He slid into the Jeep. "I have a date."

"Oh." She looked surprised. Her gaze moved to his hands resting on the steering wheel, then strayed toward the open field beyond the house.

Glad for the silence, he followed her gaze, his eyes straining to see in the dusky light. Patches of red and gold and pink wildflowers tangled throughout the tall meadow grass until the field gave way to trees. The woods weren't too thick yet. Spring had gotten a late start and all the new leaves hadn't come in, but John had no doubt that within a couple of weeks, the greenery would be dense and lush.

He shifted his attention back to the woman and watched her while she stared out at the scenery. She puzzled him. Although he knew she was the one who'd selected the lot for the house, she didn't look to be the type to live out here in the middle of nowhere. In fact, she didn't look as if she belonged in Bachelor Falls at all.

And then he remembered she was none of his business. She was marrying the guy who wrote his checks.

She turned toward him and caught him staring. He didn't so much as blink. Frowning slightly, she lifted her chin in subtle challenge. But he continued to watch her because to suddenly look away would make matters worse. Then she did that little shimmy thing again, and he knew he'd disconcerted her.

He tugged the bill of his cap down lower and eased his attention toward the fading sunset. Although he couldn't actually see the sun, salmons and pinks streaked the horizon. It really was beautiful here.

Maybe he'd hang around longer than the six months he'd planned on staying.

"We could have both saved a lot of time if you'd told me the status of the house," she said, her tone slightly huffy. "Why don't we quit playing games and set things straight right now? Then we won't have to wait for Gary and you can go on your...date."

"I have no intention of waiting." He turned the key in the ignition. "And I seem to recall already having told you about the status of the house. It won't be ready in four weeks."

She stepped away from the car when the engine roared but she put up a hand. "Wait a minute."

He'd been about to back up but reluctantly slipped the gear into Neutral and leaned back in his seat. But he wasn't going to spend the next ten minutes arguing with her. She might be used to pushing Gary around, but John wasn't about to put up with her antics.

She moved closer and peered into the Jeep, her nearness making him tense.

"What?" he asked with uncharacteristic impatience.

She jumped at the short bark, but she didn't back away. Instead she laid a hand on the windowsill, her pink-tipped fingers only a fraction from his arm. He didn't know what she was doing...except scaring the hell out of him.

"Your thumb," she said softly. "How is it?"

"My thumb?" He realized that he'd reflexively shifted away from her.

"Yeah, your thumb." She smiled, moved closer and held out her hand. "Let's see it."

Cloves. She smelled like sweet, spicy cloves.

And her blouse was still tight.

And she was leaning into his car and...

Bloody hell.

"My thumb is great." He threw the gear into Reverse. Kelly backed up and straightened. "Never better."

"Hey, we're supposed to talk about the house."

He revved the engine, then started rolling backward. The last glimpse he got of her was in his rearview mirror, her expression shooting daggers, her hands cupping shapely, heart-stopping hips.

AFTER LANA POKED and squeezed several of the chocolate morsels, she selected one, then pushed the box of candy across the kitchen table.

Glaring at her, Kelly swept the temptation aside. "You know I have to lose weight before the wedding."

She sighed and tried to pull in her stomach, her gaze wandering toward a square piece of dark chocolate with an almond sitting on top. She'd only lost three pounds so far; she didn't know how she was going to lose the last seven.

"You look fine," Lana said between licks of chocolate, making Kelly wonder what the prison sentence was for involuntary manslaughter.

"If I don't fit into that dress, I'm going to have to slit something," Kelly said, narrowing her eyes at her friend. "And we're not talking fabric here."

Lana promptly popped the remainder of the candy into her mouth and swallowed it. "Why are you being so touchy about your weight? Gary didn't say anything, did he?"

Kelly sighed. "Of course not."

Lana looked away. But Kelly already knew what she was thinking. Gary would never say boo about anything Kelly did. Anyone who didn't know him would think he simply didn't care.

He did, though, in his own way. Kelly knew that, even if her friends did think the marriage was a mistake. Although they wouldn't be so crass as to say anything negative at this point, they'd made their opinions clear when she'd first told them she was going to marry him.

Besides, a lot of women married their best friends. Hadn't Ellie done that? And everyone in Bachelor Falls could see how blissfully happy she was.

"Why were you asking about June Dale yesterday evening?" Lana asked. "I hadn't seen her in ages, but funny thing, I saw her at the movies last night. Right after you asked Ellie about her."

"You did?" Kelly looked up from the invitations she was addressing and promptly forgot about the almond-topped chocolate. She leaned back casually in her chair. "Was she with anyone?"

Lana's eyebrows rose. "Yeah, her sister. Why?"

Kelly shrugged. "Just curious."

"Are you planning on inviting her to the wedding?"

"I was thinking about it." As soon as the lie left Kelly's lips she bowed her head and concentrated on the invitations.

"Marla Higgins, too?"

Kelly looked up. "What about Marla?"

"Are you inviting her?" Lana asked, and when she frowned, Lana said, "You asked about her, too."

"Oh, yeah. I just hadn't seen her in a couple of months and I was wondering about her. That's all."

Lana nodded and pulled another stack of envelopes out of the box. "I saw her last week. She looks fabulous. I think she went to some kind of fat farm and lost about fifteen pounds. Plus she got a great haircut."

"I hate her." Kelly busied herself with checking off the guest list and tilted her head in casual inquiry. "Is she seeing anyone?"

"I wouldn't know." Lana glanced at the kitchen wall clock, then stood. "You're going to shoot me but I have to go. Blake is coming home early today and we planned a picnic dinner. I'll finish addressing these tomorrow."

"Isn't it a little brisk for a picnic?"

A wide smile stretched across Lana's face. She didn't have to say anything more. Ever since she'd met Blake she'd started smiling like that all the time.

Kelly stuffed the envelopes back in the box. Sometimes love was sickening. There was a lot to be said for marrying someone you knew most of your life. You got to skip all that giddy, syrupy stuff. Except that didn't apply to Ellie and Ross, she reminded herself, and felt her spirits sink another notch.

She sighed, unsure what was making her so moody. She was happy for both her friends. They had great husbands who made them ecstatic. Kelly herself was happy with stability.

"Go have your picnic," she said, giving her friend a smile. "I think I'll call it a day, too."

"Thanks, Kell." Lana paused at the door. "I may be a little late tomorrow. Ellie and I are stopping by

Henderson's bakery to choose the cake for your shower."

"Oh, I already swung by there and—"

Lana's shoulders drooped. "You promised."

"I'm not sticking my nose into anything."

"Yes, you are. Look, Kelly, the earth will keep rotating even if you stand still."

"I know that."

"Then, damn it, stand still, and trust Ellie and I to take care of your shower."

"Of course I trust you. It's just that..." Her voice trailed away. "It's not you. It's me. But I'm trying."

"I know you are." Lana smiled. "Hey, you haven't run across Purple Bunny yet, have you?"

"No, I was hoping you had." Uneasiness cramped Kelly's shoulders. The beloved but battered stuffed animal they'd shared since grade school was as important to any of the trio's events as cake was to a birthday party. For twenty years they'd passed him back and forth without incident. He sure picked a rotten time to play hide-and-seek with them.

Lana shook her head. "I know Ellie hasn't either, not since the day of her wedding. I spoke to her this morning. She's worried about not finding him before the shower."

Kelly cringed. It was a stupid superstition, thinking Purple Bunny would bring luck and happiness. One they should have left in childhood. Only they hadn't. And now they had to find him before she took her vows.

"He'll turn up," Lana said, but Kelly could see the misgiving in her friend's eyes. "Well, I'll see you tomorrow."

Kelly waved, then watched the door close.

Exhaling, she slouched in her chair. She really was trying to change. But basically, she'd been in charge of her life since she was eight and letting go wasn't that easy. Except how much control did she have, anyway? Real life wasn't like her job in accounting, where answers were definitive. Maybe that's why she liked being a bookkeeper so much. Seeing everything in black and white was comforting.

And so was the thought of her house. It was going to be spectacular. She'd even picked out the mailbox already, a pretty pastel yellow with a vine of pink flowers crawling along the side, which she'd painted herself. Everything was going to be perfect. Just like she'd planned.

She toyed with the edge of an envelope until it was too scuffed to use anymore, letting her mind wander, yet not finding the usual comfort she did when she pictured the house sitting serenely behind its white picket fence.

She straightened suddenly.

Ona Mae.

She would know whom John Cappel was dating. Most people in town thought the older woman was crazier than a loon. Kelly didn't share that belief. They'd become quite close over the years, and in fact, Kelly appreciated all her eccentricities. Besides, crazy or not, Ona Mae usually knew everything that went on in Bachelor Falls.

The phone was within arm's reach, and Kelly twisted around to grab it off the wall. She'd have to be careful how she broached the subject. Auntie Om, as she and her friends often called her, knew Kelly too well and Kelly didn't want to sound obvious. Then she'd have to explain herself. She frowned. Not that she *could* explain herself.

While the phone rang, she tangled the cord around her fingers. She had no business poking into John Cappel's personal life like this. What did she care about his dating habits? She didn't. Not really. Except he was supposed to be working on her house…

"Auntie Om? It's Kelly."

"You have good timing. I just finished watching 'American Bandstand.'"

Kelly grinned. "Have you had dinner yet?"

"I'm making a salad now. Why don't you come over here this time?"

Rabbit food. Kelly made a face. Although she *was* supposed to be on a diet. "Okay, I'll pick up dessert." When Ona Mae clucked her tongue in disapproval, Kelly added, "Something low fat."

"You shouldn't be roaming around after dark."

Kelly laughed. "I'm just stopping in town."

"Oh, dear, I'm not sure that's a good idea." After a pause, Ona Mae whispered into the phone, "They're back."

A chill chased down Kelly's spine at the tenseness in the other woman's voice, and she leaned forward to slide the kitchen window closed. "Who?"

"The aliens."

Chapter Three

As soon as Kelly pulled her Ford Escort in front of Jasper's Save-Rite and saw John's black Jeep, she knew she had more to worry about than a mere alien invasion.

She and Ona Mae didn't really need dessert. Kelly would fit into her wedding dress all the better, and Ona Mae...well, she was still hoping the fiancé who'd been abducted by aliens, Lowell Murtry, would return after forty-something years and was intent on staying trim enough to greet him in one of her vintage poodle skirts.

Kelly's hand hovered in the air for a moment before she turned the key with vicious disgust. The engine died and she lifted her chin to check her reflection in the mirror.

If anything, John Cappel should be afraid of running into *her*. He was the one dodging the questions. And now, since Gary had to unexpectedly go out of town for three days, John was just going to have to deal with her.

She pressed her lips together. The new magenta-colored lipstick she was wearing was awfully bright, even for her. She dabbed at it with her little finger but the tint remained stubbornly intact.

Reaching into the glove box for a tissue, she pulled out a handful of Sunshine's old incense sticks. She shook her head and made another pass through the compartment. There was lots of other useless junk, most of it belonging to her mother, but no tissues.

After taking a final glance at her reflection, Kelly slid out of the car, dropped the incense in a trash can and entered the store. Since it was already the dinner hour, the place was quiet and the aisles mostly clear.

Sometimes Old Man Jasper used an ancient intercom to play fifties music over a hum of static, but tonight you could hear a pin drop. Kelly would have welcomed any noise as she headed toward the produce section and tried not to show undue interest in the other aisles. The store wasn't that small, but it was small enough that she was bound to run into John, and she would have preferred to do that without an audience.

Everyone in Bachelor Falls knew everyone else's business. In self-defense, Kelly had quit caring what they all thought long ago, but she had Gary to consider. They all knew he was in charge of the house. And they all knew that she couldn't keep her nose out of it.

But that wasn't a reason to let John Cappel sidestep her. Or Gary.

Smoothing the fabric of her short peach linen skirt, she squeezed by the twin bubble gum machines. She knew exactly where the fresh shipment of strawberries were and Ona Mae loved them to distraction. She'd be ready to part with just about any information for a couple of the plump ripe fruits, especially this time of year when they were sometimes hard to find.

Veering to the right, Kelly hoped to avoid the checkout stand and having to stop and chat. But Thelma Perkins, sporting her ever-present beehive hairdo, craned her neck and waved as she lumbered the short distance from the cash register to the end of the counter to bag Mrs. Whipple's groceries.

Then Jasper yelled from the storeroom that Thelma's husband was on the phone and for her to hurry because he was waiting for his dinner. Thelma hollered for him to keep his shirt on, and after that Kelly was relieved to find that it was chaos as usual.

She chuckled as she listened to the interchange between the owner and his longtime employee. Anyone would think the two of them were married. But they'd known each other since childhood—they were practically like family, as were so many other people here in Bachelor Falls. Just like her and Gary.

"Why the sudden long face? I liked the smile much better."

At the sound of John's voice, Kelly blinked and looked up from the plums she'd stopped to stare at. "What?"

He mimicked her frown with a quick, teasing one of his own, then one side of his mouth hiked up. "The smile was much more becoming."

She tried to relax the sudden tension in her shoulders. "What are you doing here?"

"Shopping," he said, his dry tone communicating more than the word.

"Sorry, I didn't mean to sound abrupt. My mind was wandering and you startled me."

He nodded indifferently and started to ease past her, balancing his shopping basket in front of him. Thanks to a barrel of apples Jasper had placed at the end of the aisle, she couldn't get out of the way quickly enough.

Kelly sucked in a breath, but it was still too tight a squeeze and she brushed against him, the top of her head skimming his chin, her shoulder grazing his chest. The brief but potent contact sent her momentarily off balance and she leaned into him. Her right breast flattened against his left biceps.

The look of astonishment on his face would have been priceless if she hadn't wanted to shrivel up like a prune and roll under the cart of homegrown tomatoes.

She straightened immediately and knocked at least a dozen Granny Smiths to the floor.

"Oh, hell." She quickly dropped down to pick up the fruit, glad she didn't have to look at him.

But he crouched down, too, his knee brushing hers, his warm breath dancing across her flushed cheek.

"I can do this by myself," she said, trying to scoot back without success.

"This was my fault. I'm sorry."

She herded the apples against one knee and scooped them up, tossing one after the other into the barrel in rapid succession.

He threw in the last two, then stood and offered her a hand. She wanted to ignore it. But she had little choice other than to accept his help if she didn't want to seem rude or create a further scene.

She pushed back the tendril of hair that clung to her face, then extended her hand.

His fingers circled her wrist, and his palm pressing against her skin was slightly rough, though not un-pleasantly so. Once he'd pulled her to her feet, he didn't let go right away, but as soon as her eyes met his, they both broke contact at the same time.

"Thanks," she said, glancing away. No one had witnessed their little tango as far as she could tell. But she'd know for sure when she read the headlines of the *Bachelor Falls Gazette* tomorrow morning.

"No problem."

Her gaze strayed to his shopping basket. Two steaks, two huge baking potatoes, two ears of corn...and a pint of strawberries. Looks like it was date night again. Fine. She wouldn't keep him.

Hiking her purse up more securely on her shoulder, her gaze darted to the counter with the lone pineapple, two baskets of bruised blueberries and a pathetic-looking carton of raspberries. She frowned, returning her attention to his basket, then swept her gaze up to his face.

"Where'd you get the strawberries?" she asked.

He inclined his head toward the pineapple. "Over there. But this is the last one."

"Great."

"Wait a minute," he said, squinting at her.

"What?" She reared her head back when he nudged his face closer. "What?" she repeated when he hadn't answered.

He gestured toward her cheek. "You've got something on your face."

It was an old joke, one she'd suffered all through grammar school.

"It's a beauty mark," she said, trying to keep the

defensiveness out of her voice. It was funny how a simple remark could trigger old childhood feelings.

The litany of old taunts took a quick spin through Kelly's brain. *Kelly St. James is weird. Her mother's a hippie. They wear strange clothes. They live in a commune and don't take baths. Kelly's face is always dirty.*

"No, not that," John said, "over here." Very lightly he touched his little finger to a place closer to her ear.

Maybe he hadn't actually made contact. Possibly she sensed his touch rather than felt it, but a tingling set her nerves in motion nevertheless.

She pulled back and twisted around to use the metal bowl of a scale to see her reflection. A streak of magenta lipstick marked her face. She dabbed it away then checked her fingers. Sure enough, her little one was still smudged. She rubbed it free of color, grateful for something to do with her suddenly nervous hands.

"We still have a problem," he said while she continued to fuss with her hands.

Well, she wasn't wearing a slip, so it couldn't be showing. She slid him a wary look. "We do?"

He reached into his basket, then held up the strawberries. "We could split them."

"Or you could be a gentleman and give them to me."

His lips curved into a lazy smile. "Didn't you learn how to share?"

"Are you kidding?" She laughed, stopping herself just in time from making a crack about life in a commune. He didn't have to know about that.

"It seems the most sensible thing to do."

She eyed the fruit. "There's barely enough for three people."

He shrugged. "It's up to you, Kelly."

"Does your, uh...date eat strawberries?"

His eyebrows drew together in a quick frown. Then that same lazy smile tugged at his mouth again. "My date eats whatever I tell her to eat."

Kelly laughed, not sure if he was teasing her or not. "What rock did you crawl out from under? In this country, that attitude is called chauvinistic with a very big *C*."

His smile was gone in an instant. "I'm an American. Just like you." He started to move toward the front of the store. "At least, I presume you are."

Startled by his sudden change in mood, she stayed rooted for a few moments, then hurried after him. "Hey, we didn't decide on the strawberries yet."

"I decided."

"Okay, I'll split them with you."

"Then you'd better make it snappy. I'm checking out."

Although she didn't care much for his tone, he'd already made it to the first counter, and she had to speed up if she wanted to get her share of the berries. She reached him in time to see Thelma Perkins turn down the volume of the portable radio she had near the register and level curious brown eyes in their direction.

As he swung the basket onto the counter, her attention was drawn to the rounding of his biceps, and with vivid clarity, she remembered her right breast pressed up against it. The air felt warm suddenly and she plucked her white cotton blouse away from her skin.

His gaze briefly rested on her chest and a fresh surge of blood heated her skin as she wondered if he remembered, too.

"Are you two together?" Thelma asked, peering at them over her black cat-eye-style glasses, her eyes sparkling with both disapproval and the excitement of discovery.

"Yes," John said at the same time Kelly said, "No."

His eyebrows rose. "You decided against the strawberries?"

"No." She turned to Thelma while throwing open the flap of her purse. "I'll pay for them, then I've got to get some whipped cream."

"Hmm. Whipped cream. Why didn't I think of that?"

At his lowered, more intimate tone, Kelly stopped fishing for her wallet and darted Thelma a look. The way he'd said that had the older woman's eyes widening to the size of giant cinnamon rolls and she leaned across the counter so as not to miss another word.

Kelly gritted her teeth. Was he nuts? Didn't he know how that sounded? She gave him the evil eye, then pulled out her wallet and said, "You should try it. That's the only way Gary and I eat them."

"Isn't he out of town?" Thelma asked with a suspicious glint in her eye.

"Who?" Kelly asked with complete innocence, hoping her obtuseness would embarrass the eavesdropper. She should have known better.

"Gary, of course." Thelma frowned at John's basket, and slowly withdrew the two steaks. Her gaze raised to John's face, bounced between him and Kelly a couple of times, flicked to the pair of potatoes, then slowly slid to the two ears of corn snuggled cozily in the corner. A knowing grin started to curve her orange-ringed mouth.

Kelly would be willing to bet her new house that the gossipy cashier would be on the phone before either of them got in their respective cars.

"Could you give us an extra bag, Thelma?" she quickly asked. "A small one will do. We're splitting the strawberries."

Behind her, John chuckled. Kelly saw red. She wanted to ask him what the hell *that* meant, but she was afraid of the answer.

"I hate to rush you, Thelma, but Ona Mae is waiting dinner for me." Kelly smiled and plucked several bills from her wallet. There. That information should clarify everything.

"Oh, no." John's big hand closed around Kelly's, urging her to return the money to her purse. "Let me." He winked. "You get it next time."

Next time?

Thelma's excitement twinkled in her eyes and Kelly couldn't stand to witness another minute of it. She shoved the money back into her purse, pushed past John without saying a word and marched toward the dairy case.

Behind her, she heard Thelma whisper to him in an animated voice, "We have scented candles in the back."

KELLY CHANGED HER MIND. She didn't want to know one blessed thing about John Cappel. In fact, if she never saw him again, that would suit her fine. Except she still hadn't found out about the completion date of her house.

Sighing, she speared a piece of lettuce with her fork and dragged it across her plate. Without any salad dressing, the journey wasn't an easy one.

Ona Mae stopped pulling the little heads off her alfalfa sprouts and stared at Kelly. "Don't you like your dinner? Bet you want all that gooey, fattening blue cheese stuff on it."

"Chocolate would be better."

The older woman chuckled. "You've had a long face since you got here. If chocolate will do the trick and get you to smiling, I'll see if I can dig up some."

Kelly grinned. Ona Mae was the original health-food nut. No way did she have anything as decadent as chocolate in her house. Good thing, too. Kelly's blouses had gotten snug enough that she was on the verge of needing to buy the next size up. Which, of course, was out of the question. She'd starve herself first. Yet in the mood she was in, she could have put away half a pound of the candy in seconds flat.

"Well, missy, want to tell me what's troubling you?"

Kelly laid down her fork. If she could tell anyone, she could tell Ona Mae. Although her friend was quite active with the local grapevine, she'd never repeat Kelly's confidences. Even if she did, people in Bachelor Falls seldom listened to the resident eccentric anyway.

Impulsively, Kelly reached across the table and

briefly patted her friend's blue-veined hand. She understood her perfectly. Like Kelly, she'd been the town's outcast just because she dared to be different, dared to have her own mind.

Yet they both seemed helplessly compelled to remain in Bachelor Falls...Ona Mae, because after forty years, she still waited in vain for her Lowell to return and marry her. And Kelly, well, Kelly wasn't sure what kept her here. She only knew that once her house was finished, everything would be perfect and she wouldn't have a reason to leave.

And John Cappel wasn't going to get in her way.

By not finishing the house on time, that is.

It wasn't anything personal.

This was about the house.

Kelly took a deep breath, wondering if this was a good time to ask Ona Mae what she knew about the man. But when she raised her gaze to her friend's face, an amused gleam twinkling in the older woman's eye made Kelly reconsider. She didn't give a hoot about John Cappel.

"I guess I'm a little nervous about the wedding," Kelly hedged, shrugging. "I just want everything to go well."

Ona Mae leaned back in her chair, her posture ramrod straight as always. "Lord knows I'm no expert on weddings," she said without rancor. Kelly figured forty-something years was a long time to get over being jilted. "But I know a fair amount about cold feet and I say it's about time."

Kelly blinked. "I don't have cold feet. You know how long I've wanted this house."

Ona Mae's mouth softened, her kind hazel eyes

trained on Kelly as she leaned forward to squeeze her hand.

Kelly pressed her lips together. How could she sound so crass? Of course she was excited about becoming Gary's wife. "You know what I mean," Kelly mumbled and looked away. "I thought you were going to dig up some chocolate."

"Coming right up." Ona Mae sprinted off her chair with the energy of a woman half her age.

Kelly sighed, doubtful her friend would be successful, but nevertheless thankful for the time-out. People didn't understand about her and Gary's relationship. But it didn't matter. She and Gary were comfortable. They had similar goals and values. The success of their marriage had quite favorable statistics.

She watched Ona Mae root through the freezer compartment of the ancient refrigerator, which was only one step above an icebox. Like her assortment of poodle skirts, everything that surrounded Ona Mae was a page from the past. Her appliances were yellowing, as was the pink daisy wallpaper that covered her kitchen walls.

"Here we go." The older woman dragged out a large wad of plastic wrap and began unraveling it. After several layers were gone, she frowned at the block of ice she produced. "Did you want white, dark or milk chocolate?"

Without waiting for an answer, she poked her head in the freezer again and withdrew another package, unwrapped it and smiled. "Only two more minutes," she said over her shoulder as she rummaged through a drawer.

Uneasily, Kelly watched her friend withdraw an ice pick. Kelly hadn't seen one of those in years, but it was Ona Mae's odd behavior that had her concerned. How did she think she was going to get chocolate from ice?

"The rule is that the ice has to melt by itself before you can get to it," Ona Mae said, glancing at her, and Kelly chuckled when she finally understood what her friend was up to. "But we'll make an exception this time."

With that, she turned back to the block of ice and began chipping away with a vengeance, her frail thin body jerking and jolting with the effort.

"Ona Mae!"

"You hush, a body can't live on salad alone."

"No, I mean, maybe it would be easier if we put it on the stove." Actually, it would have been easier if they had a microwave, but that was far too modern for Ona Mae.

The older woman pursed her mouth for a moment, then switched on the front gas burner and got out a pot. "I don't do this often, you know. The whole idea is to give myself time to think about whether I really want the chocolate."

Kelly nodded. "I froze my credit cards once. But I should have gotten rid of the microwave, too."

"That's the trouble with most folks nowadays. Everything is far too convenient." She bent down to check the height of the flame and adjusted it to her liking. "Who knows, I bet by the time we get this ice melted, you may not even want any of this fattening chocolate."

Kelly gave her a bland look. "It would be safer to

bet your people from the planet Bost will show up."
Her eyes widened at the thoughtless remark and she
fought the urge to cover her mouth. "I'm sorry, Ona
Mae. You know I didn't mean anything by that."

"It doesn't matter. This time the Bostians are coming back. And I've got proof."

"Really?" Kelly asked politely. She figured she
deserved an earful after her sarcastic crack. Her gaze
wandered to the stove. At least she'd have some chocolate to help wash it down. "What's your proof?"

"They sent someone."

"The aliens?"

"No, the government." Ona Mae yanked out a
pink crocheted potholder from a drawer, then jabbed
a finger in the air. "He's working on your house. I
suppose that's his cover."

Kelly's gaze riveted to her friend's smug face.
"John Cappel?"

"That's what he calls himself."

Kelly blinked twice. Then she swallowed and
forced the corners of her mouth to stay firm. "He's
a carpenter, Ona Mae."

"Yeah?" She turned to poke a finger in the softening chocolate. "Then what's a carpenter doing getting registered mail from Uncle Sam?"

Chapter Four

Now what did she want?

John caught sight of Kelly out of his peripheral vision as he picked up his lunch sack. She'd just entered the front of the house and was obviously headed in his direction. He thought briefly about ducking out one of the windows and making a break for his Jeep. He was getting tired of his own cooking, anyway. Some potato soup from Mabel's Diner sounded better than the egg-salad sandwich he'd made himself this morning.

But the men would know that he'd turned tail and run from her just like the rest of them did. And he'd be damned if he'd let them, or her, think she intimidated him for one second.

Okay, maybe she did. The rest of the men didn't have to know that, though.

He kicked around scraps of molding, clearing a spot for himself to sit on the concrete floor, careful to not leave any room for her. Besides, he wasn't afraid of her in the same way they were. It was the little shimmy thing she did that scared the hell out of him. And the tight blouses. Why did the woman wear such snug clothes? There should be a law.

Using the wall for support, he sank down to the floor and propped the paper sack on his thighs.

"I'm glad I caught you," she said as soon as she parked herself near his boots.

"You didn't." He continued to inspect the inside of his bag without looking up.

"I mean, I was afraid you'd gone into town for lunch."

"No. I like peace and quiet while I eat."

There was a brief silence and he was tempted to look up, but he pulled out his squashed sandwich instead, and unwrapped it.

"I suppose that was a hint," she said, then dragged a sawhorse over and sat down. "What happened to your sandwich?"

He glanced up to see her frowning at his egg salad, her nose wrinkling in disgust. Then she did that shimmy thing.

Damn it.

He threw his sandwich back in the wrapper and started to stand. But she was so close he nearly knocked her off the sawhorse. She grabbed his upper arm for balance, her fingers curling around his biceps. His hand shot out to cup her waist.

"Okay?" he asked, his tone becoming gruffer than he'd intended when he realized he didn't want to let go.

"Fine," she said, straightening, and he promptly dropped his hold.

Her gaze settled on the fingers she still had

wrapped around his arm and she abruptly withdrew her hand, too.

"Look, I'm sorry I disturbed your lunch," she said, looking down at the mangled sandwich lying on the concrete floor. "In fact, I totally ruined it." Her contrite eyes met his. "Let me buy you lunch at Mabel's. She has great potato soup and homemade apple pie."

"You think that's a good idea?"

Her eyebrows drew together slightly. "Oh, maybe you're right. We could go to my place. It's not far."

He coughed. "I don't know what you're talking about, but I only meant our track record around food isn't so great."

She sighed with impatience. "I was referring to that stunt you pulled at Jasper's yesterday."

"Stunt I pulled?" He picked up his lunch sack to see what was salvageable.

"Don't bat those baby blues at me. It won't work."

He chuckled, staring at her in disbelief. "I don't bat my eyes." She stared back in defiant silence, and he added, "However, if I did, it would work."

She folded her arms across her chest. "You're not only rude but you're arrogant, too."

He nodded indifferently, and popped a strawberry into his mouth. "By the way, you were right about the whipped cream."

Her gaze grudgingly drew to the bag of leftover fruit. "I see your date didn't agree."

"Oh, she agreed," he said and carefully selected another berry. "I only let her have two. She's gotta watch her weight."

She squinted at him as if she were trying to decide

if she'd heard correctly. He did everything in his power not to laugh.

"You can't be for real," she finally said, shaking her head and letting her arms fall to her side. "We need to talk about the house."

Her voice was all business again, and he found he missed the stunned, unguarded expression that showed a different side of Kelly. It had been the uncertain side, the side that made her seem softer and more approachable.

"I thought we were waiting for Gary to get back." He reached down to make sure they hadn't damaged his boom box in their shuffle. It was old and temperamental and faded out sometimes. He hoped this wasn't one of those times. He hated working without music.

"Don't you dare turn that on."

John stopped at the sharpness in her tone. Slowly he looked up. "Excuse me?"

Her chin lifted, her cheeks were slightly flushed and anger flashed across her face. But it was too late. He'd already seen the unexpected spark of fear that had darkened her topaz eyes, and his own sudden irritation with her uncalled-for abruptness lessened.

Her tongue darted out to moisten her lips. "Please, give me a minute. Don't dismiss me like that."

He finished what he'd started out to do by giving the boom box a small shake. The low hum of the oldies station he listened to sprang to life.

"It was already on," he said, without taking his eyes off her. "I just wanted to make sure it was still working." He left the volume low, so low that it was barely audible.

"I'm sorry." She drew a hand up her opposite arm and looked past him. "I shouldn't have snapped like that."

"Sit down," he said, sliding to one side of the sawhorse, knowing he was going to regret the offer. He didn't even know why it popped out of his mouth.

She hesitated, and glanced over her shoulder. The men had already dispersed, most of them heading into town for lunch. Simon didn't generally go with the rest of them, but he'd already disappeared into the woods to down his usual beer he thought the rest of them didn't know about. And Dusty had yet to return from picking up their order of nails.

Gingerly she sat at the other end of the sawhorse. Still, there wasn't much room between them and John could smell the fragrance clinging to her hair. It reminded him of cloves. The really sweet kind his mom used to cook with before she got too sick.

She rubbed a hand down her thigh, smoothing out the pale pink fabric of her slacks. She was nervous. For some strange reason, so was he. "When do you think the house will be completed?"

"I'm guessing July."

Her shoulders sagged. "The beginning or end?"

"End."

Her sigh was deep. "What if we hired more men?"

Maybe it was the slump in her posture or the slight echo of defeat he heard in her voice, but he genuinely felt bad that he couldn't give her better news. "Look, I know you're disappointed you can't spend your wedding night here, but—"

She nearly growled. "Would you quit talking about

my wedding night? That has nothing to do with anything.''

"Easy.'' He reared back. "I figured—''

She stood, waving a hand. "Don't figure. Just hammer.''

Any sympathy he'd felt evaporated. "So the bottom line is, you just want your way. And you don't care who has to break their back to make sure you get it.''

"I don't see anyone breaking their back. In fact, if a certain someone wasn't so busy chasing down strawberries for his dates, that someone could be getting his work done like his contract stipulates.''

She really could be a witch. He shook his head and stared. The sun streamed in from behind her, making it hard to see her face clearly, so when he thought he saw tears glistening from her eyes, he figured the light was playing tricks on him. He angled for a better look but she turned away.

"I'm not trying to be difficult,'' she said, her voice sounding reasonably steady. "And I'm not trying to get my way. It's just that...'' Her voice trailed off and she made an annoyed sweep through the air with her hand as she searched for the right words. "I'm superstitious. Everything has to be on time and perfect for this wedding. It's bad enough that we can't find Purple Bunny. He always brings me luck.''

"If you're relying on luck to make a marriage work, you'd better think twice about it.''

She spun around and pinned him with an incredulous stare. He deserved every uncomfortable second of it. He had no business making remarks about the probable success or failure of her marriage.

"I suppose you believe in the legend of the falls, too," he said to bridge the silence. It was a safe topic. Apparently the entire town was superstitious about their annual Bachelor Daze festival determining the town's upcoming nuptials.

"Not really." A small smile played at the corners of her mouth. "Did you go to the festival? It's a lot of fun. All the single men head for the falls with the married guys helping them, while the women try to block their paths. No bachelor who takes a dip in the falls will be married during the following year. We had it a few weeks ago." She shrugged. "Ellie and Ross sort of threw a wrench in the works by getting married. But most people figure that didn't count since they showered togethered. Anyway, we don't *all* believe in it."

Suddenly remembering something, John shifted uneasily. He truly hoped she didn't.

He rubbed the back of his neck. "Okay, back to the house. I want to get this job over with, too. I can't stick around all summer." Not true. He'd planned on staying through fall.

She started at his abrupt change in tone. That earlier unguarded expression returned and made her face look young and vulnerable again. "You're leaving?"

Surely she wasn't sorry to see him go. "Mayor Bartlett has a small job for me in his office, then I'll be hitting the road."

Her expression tightened. "Must be nice to be foot-loose and fancy-free."

"It is," he agreed, which produced two lines of tension on either side of her mouth.

"This house is important to me. What can we do to get back on schedule?"

"Have dinner with me," he said. If he'd intentionally tried to shock her, he couldn't have done a better job. Her eyes widened and her lips parted, but no sound came out. "Or if that isn't convenient, maybe we could meet over a cup of coffee after it gets dark."

"After it gets dark?" The sudden wariness narrowing her eyes was almost comical.

"When it's too late to work anymore."

She nodded. "I knew that."

"Of course you did," he said, reaching for his hammer and swallowing back a grin. "So what's it going to be, because right now I need to get back to work."

"Dinner. No, coffee. Let's make it coffee." She chewed at her lower lip, then nodded absently. "We'll meet at Mabel's. Is seven okay?"

"Seven it is."

"Wear jeans," she said, and when he turned to look quizzically at her, she added, "What you have on is fine. What I mean is, don't get dressed up or anything."

No, what she meant was—make this look like a business meeting. "I wouldn't dream of it."

"Yes." Her gaze raked a path over his faded navy blue T-shirt down to his even more disreputable jeans sporting a slash several inches above the knee. "I'm sure you wouldn't."

John didn't take offense. Although he might have if she hadn't moistened her lips as her gaze lingered on his chest. Instead, the subtle reaction gave him enormous satisfaction...and a very masculine response.

He shifted uncomfortably and cursed under his breath.

He didn't need her checking out his jeans again.

And he didn't need to be having this reaction. Bloody hell, she was about to marry Gary Sizemore.

He patted his breast pocket in search of a nail while his other hand tightened around the hammer. He turned away from her. They didn't have anything more to say right now. She needed to get her fanny on the road, and he needed to get back to work.

But she didn't get the hint. She stayed where she was, staring at him, and like a fool, his gaze drew back to her.

As irritated as it made him, his attention immediately landed on the snug fit of her blouse across her chest. The pale pink fabric was almost sheer and faintly traced something lacy beneath. Quickly he switched his gaze to her face.

Open curiosity brightened her eyes and captured his fascination like no other part of her anatomy could. Then, as if she realized she was staring, her brows furrowed, her topaz eyes darkening, and she looked confused, defiant and wary all at once.

Hell, he knew the feeling.

God, he wished she'd leave.

A short bark of static sprang from the boom box signaling another one of its episodes, before the faint hum of an old rock tune underscored the silence.

John stared at the radio a moment, then slowly bent over and turned up the volume.

Music split the air, echoing off the nearly finished

walls of the house. They couldn't have carried on a conversation if they wanted to.

Against his better judgment, he glanced at Kelly.

Anger, then pain, shadowed her face as she turned and walked away.

LAYING ON HER BED, Kelly stared at the handmade ceramic clock that hung on the wall above her grandmother's armoire. Sunshine had made the clock and given it to Kelly for her tenth birthday. It was years before Kelly understood why she couldn't have a Barbie or play makeup like all her friends received for their birthdays.

In fact, the only store-bought gifts she'd ever gotten were from her grandmother, Ellie, Lana or Gary. Sunshine never had any money. The few bucks she did make from her pottery always went back into the commune coffers.

Kelly hated that clock. She didn't know why she'd hung the shapeless blob. It was gray and ugly and rarely kept decent time. But Sunshine had signed the corner and Kelly somehow felt obligated to keep it.

She missed her mother sometimes, although she was glad Sunshine was happy living in Florida. The woman had often had trouble keeping her head out of the clouds but she had been fun. At least most of Kelly's friends thought so. Their lives had been dull in comparison, whereas Kelly's had been filled with interesting, well-traveled people, rock music and freedom. Lots of freedom. Too much freedom. More than any child should have.

Kelly wasn't about to make the same mistake. Her kids were going to have well-ordered, structured lives.

They would never doubt that she loved them. They would be her primary concern. The only way her kids were going to understand the word *lonely* was if they looked it up in the dictionary.

And when her kids wanted to talk, they'd have her full attention, without having to compete with the local rock station or the volume button of a stereo.

She didn't know why all these thoughts were bouncing around her head. With the wedding only three and a half weeks away, she had more to worry about than...

John.

She forced herself to unclench her teeth. She'd been in a funky mood ever since she'd returned from talking with him, and it didn't help that he'd kept popping into her head for the past two hours. Well, it wasn't *him,* personally, who had her stirred up.

Although he had ticked her off by turning up the radio, it was the house not getting finished on time that was upsetting her. Plus she was tired.

Stretching, she thought briefly about taking a nap. She'd stayed up late working on Jasper's books. The man had no mind for business. It was a miracle he'd successfully run his grocery store for a quarter of a century. But he had, and now he trusted her to keep his books.

Just like Virgil Henderson, Mabel and many of the other Bachelor Falls businesspeople. Some of them thought she was too headstrong and independent, and she figured that behind her back they'd probably criticized the way she dressed and the blond phase she'd gone through. But they trusted her and that was enough for Kelly.

She wasn't even sure if Ellie and Lana had totally understood her youthful need to reinvent herself, to adopt a glamorous image. But that was okay, too. They had always been supportive.

Until she'd told them she was marrying Gary.

She rolled over onto her stomach, and hugging her pillow, she stared into her open closet, wondering what she should wear to Mabel's Diner tonight. A strange flutter tickled the inside of her chest, making her thoughts scatter.

The sensation had nothing to do with John, and it chafed that the notion even occurred to her. It was the old tapes she was playing in her head that were the problem. She had to stop them.

Besides, her friends were wrong. Gary was going to make the perfect husband.

He'd hardly require any attention at all.

Chapter Five

"Sorry, girl, but you're on your own tonight."

John cringed when he crouched down to pet Goldie and realized how stiff his only pair of unfaded jeans were. He'd put too much starch in them. Again.

He knew better. But he'd starched them without thinking. Some habits were hard to break, as he'd found in the last year.

The golden retriever licked John's neck and whimpered.

John reared back, laughing, and narrowly missed getting his face slobbered on.

"Yeah, you have such a tough life." He opened his hand and the dog greedily slurped up the last strawberry. "Okay, that's it. They're all gone."

Goldie nudged his wrist as if she didn't believe him, and he splayed his fingers, showing her his empty palm. "You know you don't get more than two."

She watched him with rueful brown eyes as he stood.

"You got half my steak, didn't you?" he asked, but she showed no signs of remorse. He was the one who should feel remorse. He had no business giving her people food. But ever since he'd found her half-starved and filthy with neglect, he'd had a hard time refusing her anything.

Still, he wasn't doing her any favors and from now on he resolved he'd quit buying two of everything.

He gave her one last pat on the head and left the house without locking the door. Even though the cabin he was renting was only fifteen minutes from town, it was fairly isolated. Still, he never locked it, and left most of the windows open now that it had gotten warm. He liked Bachelor Falls. He'd even thought about staying longer. But in the past few days he'd started to think that might not be a good idea.

The ride into town was pleasant with the wind whipping through his Jeep. After he pulled into a parking stall in front of Mabel's Diner, he checked his reflection in the rearview mirror and ran a hand over his messed-up hair. It was long, maybe a little too long. Something else he hadn't quite gotten used to.

There weren't many cars on the street and he recognized Kelly's red compact right away. He wasn't surprised that she was prompt. If she were late, she'd have to apologize and Kelly wouldn't want to have to do that.

She was a little tyrant when she wanted to be. He wouldn't be surprised if her family owned the town, or at least owned the big white pillared house at the top of the hill overlooking the falls. She was used to having her way. No doubt about it. Gary was paying him a lot of money to make sure everything was just perfect with the house. Just the way Kelly wanted it.

It irked him that he could be attracted to her at all. Not just because of Gary, but because he liked team players. And Kelly obviously wasn't one.

Which was good. Because their relationship had to be strictly business.

Although it was the dinner hour, only three tables were occupied in the diner. A couple pairs of teen-agers sat in two of the booths, heads bent close, obliv-ious to their surroundings. In the third one, Kelly sat across from Mabel, an ancient ledger spread out on the table between them.

Kelly was vigorously shaking her head. Mabel had one hand on her narrow hip as she peered at Kelly over her red-framed glasses. They were clearly having a disagreement over something. John smiled wryly to himself. His money was on Kelly and her one-track mind.

He hesitated near the door. They hadn't seen him, so he stopped to glance at the headlines of the local paper sitting on the counter, hoping to give them an-other couple of minutes.

But his gaze didn't stay on the newspaper. It kept drawing back to Kelly and the way she was leaning across the table, listening intently to the older woman.

Her hair fell slightly forward, glossy and thick, and although he hadn't noticed before she had a nearly perfect profile. Her nose was just the right proportion to her chin and high cheekbones, and her lips were tinted a pale peach. She still wore too much makeup for his taste, but it didn't disguise how truly pretty she was.

Still, what really held his attention was the way she gave her unconditional attention to Mabel. Even though it was clear she didn't agree with the woman, she listened with patience, never interrupting, never losing eye contact. That surprised him. He'd expected her to be more of a hothead.

Two teenagers started giving him funny looks and he realized that he'd been staring too long. He moved away from the counter and slowly made his way toward the booth where the two women continued to talk.

"We've done your bookkeeping the same way for six years. Why do you want to change now?" Kelly asked, her tone soft and composed.

"Hazel says she does it the other way," Mabel said, her voice not so reasonable.

"Hazel isn't my client. What she's doing is illegal. And as much as I don't want to see her get in the doghouse with Uncle Sam, I'm more concerned about you."

Kelly must have seen him out of the corner of her eye because she abruptly sat back and closed the ledger. "Let's talk about this later."

Mabel grunted and shot him a sidelong glance as she started to slide out of the red vinyl booth. "You two eating?"

"I'm not." Kelly raised her eyebrows at him.

"I ate. Coffee would be good." He smiled at Mabel. "You make the best cup in five states."

A reluctant smile curved Mabel's withered lips and she shoved at his shoulder. "Go on." She waited until he took her place in the booth, then she bowed down and whispered, "You want some of that hazelnut creamer I keep in the back?"

John winked. "Too bad you're already married, luv."

She let out a loud chortle and shoved at his shoulder again before hurrying behind the counter.

When he looked back at Kelly, an amused expression lifted one side of her mouth. "Well, well, aren't we the goodwill ambassador of Bachelor Falls? I haven't seen Mabel smile so much since her mother-in-law got laryngitis five years ago."

He shrugged. "I get tired of my own cooking. I come in a lot."

Kelly continued to stare pensively at him. "You sounded very British for a moment."

He frowned. He thought he'd lost the accent. Not particularly interested in embarking on a conversation about himself, he eyed the dog-eared ledger pages that had turned yellow with age. "You still keep books that way?"

She shook her head. "I do it on a computer," she said, lowering the pitch of her voice and glancing over her shoulder toward the kitchen. "Then I transfer the numbers to the ledger. Mabel gets too hyper trying to read a computer printout."

"Do you do that for all your clients?"

She smiled. "Only half of them."

"Is that how you met Gary?"

A puzzled frown replaced the smile. "Doing his books?"

He laughed. "No. I meant since he's an accountant, too."

"Oh." The grin was back, lighting up her eyes, making her way too attractive. "No. I've known Gary forever. We're practically like—"

Cutting herself off, she leaned farther back in her seat even though there was no place to go. Her cheeks grew as rosy as two apples and when she flipped her hair back, he noticed that her hand was a little unsteady.

She cleared her throat, and deposited the ledger into the briefcase sitting beside her. "Okay, let's discuss the house."

So, it was back to business. Which was fine with him. However, he suspected he knew what she'd been about to say. And he wasn't surprised. He'd tossed back a couple of beers with Gary a time or two, and it hadn't taken much alcohol for the guy's tongue to loosen up.

He hadn't said anything blatant or derogatory about his relationship with Kelly. Just enough to tell John the poor guy had cold feet. Ice-cold feet.

John wondered if Kelly knew about the dip Gary had taken at the Bachelor Daze festival. Of course she'd claimed she didn't believe in the superstition....

"The house?" She ducked her head, bringing her face in line with his, trying to get his attention.

He frowned, realizing his mind had wandered. "What's with the purple bunny?"

"What do you know about him?" Her voice rose in indignation and two kids in the nearby booth turned and stared. She flicked a glance their way then in a softer but firm tone, she asked, "What do you know about Purple Bunny?"

"I don't even know what a purple bunny is. I just recalled you talking about it."

Mabel walked up with their coffee. "Did you find that little rascal yet?"

"No." Kelly skewered John with an accusing look. He turned up a palm. "What?"

Mabel set down two mugs along with the hazelnut creamer. "That ain't a good sign, girlie. You can't be thinking you can go through with the wedding without him."

"Why? Is he the best man?" John grinned. Neither of the women joined him.

"Who had it last?" Mabel asked. "Lana?"

Kelly shook her head, her forehead puckered with worry lines. "Ellie did. It was right after she got married last month that we realized he was missing."

John drummed his fingers on the table, resigned to the fact that no one was going to enlighten him about the mysterious stranger.

Mabel and Kelly absently watched the motion of his hand. Finally Mabel said, "I bet that crazy old Ona Mae has him. Probably mistook him for one of her dang aliens and has him locked up in her basement." She started laughing so hard, she had to pick up the corner of her coffee-stained white apron and dry her eyes.

Kelly's mouth formed into a disapproving pout. "Don't make fun of her like that."

Mabel stepped back and out of Kelly's vision she looked meaningfully at John and made a circular motion with her forefinger near her temple, mouthing, "The woman is loco." Aloud she asked, "You two want anything besides coffee?"

Kelly sighed. "Maybe I'll have a small wedge of your apple pie."

Mabel frowned. "Does that wedding dress of yours fit yet?"

Kelly's eyes widened at the other woman, then her gaze shot to John. He looked down at his fingers and continued drumming, doing his damnedest to keep a grin in check. He didn't know what silently transpired between the two women after that, but Mabel slunk away from the table without uttering another word.

When he looked up, Kelly's expression looked so murderous that he burst out laughing. "Does everyone know everything in this town?"

"Yeah, except where Purple Bunny is." She briefly closed her eyes and massaged her left temple.

"What the devil is a purple bunny?"

"A raggedy old stuffed animal that should have been thrown out fifteen years ago." Her lips curved in a wry smile. "But my friends and I can't seem to part with him."

"So what does he have to do with your wedding?"

Silence stretched as her chin lifted and wariness crept across her face. "You wouldn't understand," she said finally. "You apparently don't believe in luck or superstition."

More importantly, he hoped she didn't. Still, he was sorry he'd made the earlier remark about the success of her marriage. "I believe in luck. We define it differently."

Her eyebrows arched. "I'm listening."

"I heard something once that makes a lot of sense to me. Luck is preparedness meeting opportunity."

She stared pensively off to the right while she considered his words, glancing absently at two couples who had just entered the diner. They both waved at her and eyed him curiously.

Mabel never did come back with Kelly's apple pie.

He didn't know if she'd forgotten or was just too busy. The place had really started filling up since he'd arrived, and the newcomers had Mabel hopping.

"I agree with that. It makes sense to me." Kelly picked up her mug and took a long thoughtful sip of coffee. Setting it down, she said, "Take marriage, for instance, or when you're deciding on a career. First, you're presented with an opportunity, then you weigh the pros and cons, analyze your options and make the best decision you can based on the information." She half smiled. "Then everyone says that you're so lucky you found Mr. Right or that you have such a great job. Baloney. They can call it luck if they want."

John frowned. Had Mabel spiked the coffee? He took a cautious sip, then stirred in more creamer. "Okay."

"What's that supposed to mean?"

He shrugged. "I never really thought about approaching marriage that way."

Her chin rose in that defensive way again. "Have you ever been married?"

"No."

"Ever thought about it?"

"Once or twice. For five minutes."

Her chin came down and her face lapsed into a puzzled expression. "Why does it turn you off?"

"I didn't say it did."

She gave him a bland look.

He exhaled and leaned back. This wasn't a conversation he wanted to get into. He had no deep dark secrets or checkered past. He just didn't want to analyze past choices he'd made. "I've moved around a lot and I didn't think it was fair to ask someone to uproot every couple of years.''

She cocked her head slightly to the side and in a grudging tone, she said, ''Well, I suppose that was a pretty responsible attitude.''

''Glad you approve.''

Her eyes abruptly met his. ''I wasn't judging you. I just didn't...'' Her voice trailed off and she sat there looking a little sheepish.

''Expect me to be so responsible?''

Her lashes lowered, giving him his answer. Then she turned away and tried to get Mabel's attention.

He should probably let her off the hook. He traced the rim of his mug with his thumb. ''How did you get that impression of me?''

''I didn't. It's just that you're different.'' She glanced around the room. ''You know how people are around here. They're born in Bachelor Falls and they die here. And they know everyone else's business in between.''

''What does that have to do with your thinking I'm irresponsible?''

''That was your word, not mine.'' She exhaled deeply. ''As boring as these people sound, they are typical and there's nothing wrong with the way they feel or live. There's comfort in knowing your surroundings and neighbors. Stability isn't a bad thing.''

''I'm very stable. Wherever I am.''

She didn't believe that. It showed in the indulgent way her lips curved.

It didn't matter to him. He was through proving himself to the world. He'd leave that kind of energy-draining futility to younger, more foolishly optimistic men.

"You still think I'm judging you, but believe me, I'd be the last person in Bachelor Falls to do that."

"Okay." He'd be a damned fool not to leave this conversation alone. "But for the sake of argument, according to your..." He gestured with his hand, searching for the appropriate word. "Formula. Could I be a husband candidate for you?"

Mabel chose that moment to appear and refill their mugs. But at his last statement, she looked up at his face and the stream of coffee missed his cup by two inches.

Kelly made a sound of disgust and pulled a wad of napkins from the dispenser to soak up the dark brew. Ignoring her, Mabel set the carafe down on the table, and swatted Kelly's hip with the back of her hand.

"Move over," she said, and slid in the booth beside Kelly. She threw up a gnarled hand at John. "Well, go on."

"Damn it, Mabel." Kelly was wedged against her briefcase on the other side.

The older woman gave Kelly a disapproving scowl. "Don't talk your commune trash talk in here." She promptly returned her attention to John. "Well?"

Commune? What was that about? John watched Kelly roll her eyes toward the ceiling. She didn't react much more than that, but he could tell she hadn't liked the comment.

"At least I don't eavesdrop," she said.

Mabel shot her a nonplussed look. "This is a public place, ain't it?"

John laughed.

Both women stared at him. Then a customer across the restaurant hollered for her potato soup and, grumbling, Mabel reluctantly slid out of the booth.

"Coming here was a bad idea." Kelly slumped against the red vinyl seat. Letting her head fall back, she stared at the ceiling. "I don't know what I was thinking."

"That it was safe."

She straightened and peered at him with narrowed eyes.

"Because if we'd met at your place, you knew that people would think there was a little hanky-panky going on between us." He paused to sip his lukewarm coffee. "Know why?"

"You'll tell me, I'm sure." Although she said it in a bored voice, she glanced nervously at Mabel taking an order four booths away.

"Despite the nice, neat little formulas you depend on…" he drawled, pausing, his gaze dropping to her mouth.

She drew in her lower lip, her straight white teeth digging into the peach-tinted flesh.

A slow, satisfied smile tugged at his mouth, and he raised his gaze until his eyes held hers for several long moments. "There's this annoying little thing called chemistry."

She blinked. "Never liked the subject."

"You don't have to."

She adjusted the shoulders of her yellow linen jacket, her gaze skimming the room. "Why would any of these people believe for one minute that we were anything but…but—"

Her attention skittered back to rest on his chest,

before roaming his shoulders, lingering on his mouth, and finally meeting his eyes.

Under her breath, she let out a short frustrated shriek. "You are so damned arrogant."

Grinning, he held up a hand, asking for patience. "So, you would never think of me in those terms?"

She wanted to deny it. He could almost see the struggle in her eyes. She reached out and moved the creamer a fraction, allowing the action to draw her concentration.

"No," she said softly but without a trace of conviction.

"Look, this isn't personal. I'm trying to prove a point."

She looked up. "Which is?"

"Marriage or choosing a mate isn't a simple recipe. Love has to enter the equation or you don't stand a chance."

Her eyes widened in surprise, anger, alarm...he didn't know which. But she couldn't possibly be half as shocked as he was at the stuff coming out of his mouth. When the hell had he become her damn guidance counselor?

"You jumped from chemistry to love?"

He exhaled. God, he was an idiot for starting this. "Let's drop it."

"No, I want to understand this." Clearly she smelled blood. She leaned forward expectantly, amusement lifting one side of her mouth.

"Chemistry, temptation, whatever you want to call it, is always going to be a problem unless you're emotionally committed to the other person."

She wrinkled her nose. "I'm not sure I follow

you.'' She brought her coffee cup to her lips but he'd already seen the smirk she was trying to hide.

"Okay, let's see if I can put it in simpler terms. Do you think we'd jump each other's bones if given the—"

Mabel bumped the table in her haste, making the coffee slosh over the rim of John's mug.

"Did I miss anything?" she asked as she reclaimed her seat beside Kelly, who looked as though she was ready to pop a major blood vessel.

John smiled at the older woman. "Good, you're back. Maybe you can settle something for us."

Chapter Six

Surely he was joking. Kelly sent him a furious look. "I don't think Mabel has time for your childish speculations," she said as she tried to nudge the woman out of the booth. "Look, Ida is trying to signal for more coffee."

"She doesn't need any more caffeine. That woman talks more than a magpie as it is." Mabel held her ground, and stared expectantly at John.

He was enjoying this, the bum. Kelly glared at him in warning but he stretched one arm out along the back of the booth, looking calm and relaxed, as though he didn't give a fig about the tension he was causing.

Maybe he only meant to tease her, Kelly thought, but he didn't know Mabel. She wasn't going to let his comment slide. She could be like a pit bull with a T-bone if she wanted to know something. And for her, this piece of gossip could end up being juicier than a slab of prime rib.

"Well," the older woman barked in a short impatient tone, then glanced at the door when it opened. Belinda Morgan walked in with her new boyfriend,

Tom, and frowned at all the occupied tables. Mabel's eyes squinted with frustration as she turned back to John. "I ain't got all night."

"Where's Henrietta this evening?" Kelly asked, trying to distract her, knowing the waitress always took Thursdays off.

"Hey, Mabel, you killing the cow or what?" Bobby Earl Jenkins sat two booths down, a fork in one hand, a napkin tucked into the neck of his faded green T-shirt and nothing but a bottle of ketchup in front of him.

"Keep your pants on," Mabel hollered at him. "Or I'll tell Mary you're sneaking burgers after supper." She shook her head and started to slide out of the booth. "Even after twenty-three years, the dang fool still can't stomach his wife's cooking."

Kelly let out a relieved sigh. As soon as Mabel got busy again, Kelly was going to hustle Big Mouth out of here.

"You two don't go nowhere. I'll be right back," Mabel said as she pulled the pencil out from behind her ear and spun toward a table of hungry-looking teenagers.

"Right," Kelly mumbled, but as soon as the other woman was out of earshot, she said, "Get up. We're leaving."

He raised his eyebrows in innocence. "But you told Mabel—"

"Get your rear end off that seat." She grabbed her wallet out of her purse, then reached for her briefcase.

"How could I refuse such a charming request?" he said, a lazy grin starting to turn up the corners of his mouth. Except he didn't move. His arm was still stretched out across the back of the booth, his biceps pushing up the fabric of his T-shirt.

The well-washed cotton molded to the muscled contours of his chest, and hugged his stomach which was enviably flat, even with his shirt tucked into those tight jeans. And his...

Her gaze skidded up to meet his watchful one. His eyes were dark, so dark that they barely looked blue. "You're proving my point," he said.

Her breath came out in a rush. "Get up right now," she said in a low, tight voice, and with a glare she hoped could frighten the devil himself.

"Are you leaving?" Belinda's hopeful voice came from behind her.

Kelly turned to assure her they were, but Mabel sidled up and said, "They're not going anywhere. They're here to talk about Kelly's house." She bounced a frown from Kelly to John. "You ain't got to that part yet, have ya?"

John laughed.

Kelly silently counted to ten. Why did she stay here in Bachelor Falls? This entire town was a joke. Privacy was nonexistent. The rumor mill was the largest employer. Kelly had liked it out West where she'd attended college. Why hadn't she stayed there?

After the brief silence, John moved, lowering his arm to the table, and the knot in Kelly's stomach started to unravel.

"We aren't leaving," he said to Belinda, "but Kelly was just coming around to make room for you two while you wait for a table." He patted the seat beside him.

"Wow, Kelly, thanks." Belinda gave her an odd

look and slid into the seat opposite John. Her boyfriend mumbled something and followed her.

Kelly shook her head. When had she lost control of her life? She sent John a nasty look. It would serve him right if she left him here with Bubblehead Belinda and Tom, who Kelly doubted could string more than two sentences together at a time. Except she didn't know if she could trust John to keep his mouth shut once Mabel put the screws to him.

After a meaningful pause that only John would notice, she settled beside him while Mabel kept the other two busy by reciting a list of specials. The items never changed. Kelly had no idea why Mabel even insisted on calling them specials. But Belinda sat entranced even though she had to know them all by heart.

And that was only one of the reasons everyone at Bachelor Falls High had called her Bubblehead since kindergarten.

"You don't mind sitting next to me, do you?" John whispered, his warm breath tickling her ear.

"Why would I?" She rubbed the side of her neck.

"No reason."

"I know what you're doing."

"Yeah?"

She heard the grin in his voice but she refused to look at him. Instead, she stared across the table at Belinda's profile as Mabel explained how they battered the chicken-fried steak.

"You're trying to distract me from talking about the house," she said in a low, accusing voice.

He said something, but with all the noise from the other diners, she couldn't hear and had to tilt her head closer to him. Again his warm breath brushed the side of her face. His shoulder dipped toward her, and his thigh pressed hers.

"I said, why would I do that?"

It had grown terribly warm with so many people packed into the place and Kelly loosened the collar of her linen shirt. She shifted closer to the edge of the bench seat away from John. "For obvious reasons."

"Not to me. I already told you it wouldn't be finished in time for your wedding night."

"Why are you so damn fixated on my wedding night?" she ground out and was irritated to find three additional pairs of eyes on her. Huffing out an exasperated breath, she barked, "What?"

Abruptly the three pairs of eyes darted away and Mabel promptly got back to the specials.

John chuckled. "Oh, I get it. You think you can bully me into a different answer."

"I'm asking you to keep your end of the bargain."

"I always do that."

Kelly shifted another inch away. It was hard to have a meaningful discussion when you had to whisper. Even harder when making eye contact brought you practically lip to lip. She glanced around the room. Wasn't anyone else warm in here?

As soon as Mabel flipped her order book closed and moved away, Belinda cleared her throat, and Kelly reluctantly looked at the blonde. Not a dark root in sight. Her hair color was all natural. Another reason not to like her.

"Kelly isn't a bully," Belinda said to John, an indignant clip to her tone. She stared at him for a moment, then lowered her gaze as color flooded her face. "I couldn't help but overhear."

A feather could have knocked Kelly over. Her mind scrambled to find something to break the brief silence, but she was so blown away by Belinda's comment that she couldn't seem to gather her thoughts fast enough.

John smiled. "I didn't mean to offend Kelly. It's sort of a joke between us."

He glanced at Kelly, and she was surprised to find uncertainty in his eyes.

Recovering her composure, she laughed and waved a hand. "Don't worry, Belinda, I never listen to a thing he says."

The other woman looked up, a tight wistful smile beginning to curve her lips. "I've always envied that about you. No matter how much they taunted you, you never seemed to care."

"Is this going to end up being chick talk?" Tom asked, rubbing his too-square jaw and sinking against the back of his seat.

This time it was Kelly's turn to squirm. She knew what Belinda was talking about, but she also knew that being newcomers, Tom and John wouldn't. She hoped Belinda didn't feel compelled to explain.

"Did you two already order?" she quickly asked. "I had the meat loaf last Monday. Mabel's trying a new recipe, hoping to compete with Hazel. It was really good."

Belinda's cute, perfect little nose wrinkled. "I thought you were on a diet?"

John laughed.

Kelly threw up a hand. "Maybe I ought to take out

an ad in the *Gazette* just in case someone didn't hear about it."

Tom shook his head in disgust. "I knew this was going to turn into chick talk."

"Oh, sit on it and spin, Tom. You think I'm not sick of hearing about crummy car engines?"

Kelly swallowed back a huge lump of surprise, but she wasn't quick enough to stifle a grin. She stared at Belinda with open admiration. The ditzy, easily led blonde who Kelly had once known had developed a backbone.

Belinda beamed back at her. "I don't think you need a diet, by the way. I just heard that you're trying to fit into your mom's dress." She shrugged. "How is Sunshine? Is she coming up from Florida for the wedding?"

"She says she is."

"She'll be surprised at your new house, won't she? I heard from Shorty that it looks a lot like Daddy's house."

Kelly straightened. "It doesn't look at all like your folk's house. I designed most of it myself."

Belinda frowned and turned to John. "You're working on it, aren't you? Don't you think it looks a lot like our house? You know, the white one at the top of the hill?"

Tom perked up. He looked from John to Kelly, back to John. "That house they're working on near Potter's field belongs to you guys? Cool. I was looking for a job. Need anyone?"

"What kind of carpentry experience have you got?" John asked. "You know anything about finishing work?"

"Wait a minute," Kelly cut in. "That's my house you're talking about."

John lifted one bemused brow. "I thought you were anxious to get it finished. Maybe we can use Tom."

He was right, of course. She nodded curtly.

Belinda laughed. "Kelly likes to do things her way."

"Yeah?"

Kelly ignored the amused sarcasm in John's voice and looked at Tom, waiting for him to answer.

"Well, actually I know more about cars," he said, shrugging his broad shoulders, a hangdog expression on his handsome face.

Except for his black hair, Tom looked a lot like Belinda's last boyfriend, and the one before that. She always seemed to choose the ones who looked like the captain of the football team. Of course, with her looks and her daddy's money, she usually got any guy she wanted.

"Tell you what." John rubbed the side of his jaw. "Without your having experience, I can't use you at the house at this stage, but my Jeep's been acting strange lately. Want to take a look at it and give me an estimate on how much it would cost to fix it?"

"Cool. Tomorrow?"

"Tomorrow's good."

Frowning, Kelly turned to John. She'd forgotten how close he was and her thoughts faltered, the words sticking in her throat. She realized she'd hesitated too long when his left eyebrow hiked up as he peered back at her.

"Can't he do *anything* to speed things up at the house?" she asked, the words coming out too sharp.

"It would take longer to show him what to do. Besides, you have too much specialty trim and molding you want done in the foyer and over the doorways."

"See," Belinda cut in. "It sounds like Daddy's house. Can I come out and see it?"

Kelly stared at the woman. Had she subconsciously patterned her house after the Morgans' home? Maybe she had. Belinda's family had always seemed to have it all—her dad worked, her mom stayed home and baked the best oatmeal raisin cookies in town. All three of the girls had always worn pretty starched dresses in lovely pastel colors. No tie-dyed hand-me-downs for them.

"Well, can I?" Impatience flickered in Belinda's wide blue eyes.

For a moment, Kelly didn't know what to say. She simply stared, her thoughts scattering like fall leaves in a windstorm. She really had copied the Morgan house. She hadn't meant to, but...

John held up a hand. "Sorry, but we're already behind schedule. Kelly will have plenty of time to show you her house when it's completed."

Belinda's lip stuck out in the familiar pout Kelly remembered from as far back as the little blond girl's fourth birthday party when Kelly had seen the Morgan house for the first time. And knew she wanted it....

She felt her hand being squeezed and realized she was staring again. Her brain briefly registered Belinda's confused expression before Kelly looked down at the small hidden space between her and John.

On the red vinyl seat, her hand lay clenched into a fist. Atop it, John's hand closed one more time in a reassuring squeeze before withdrawing and returning to his coffee cup.

It was a small, nonthreatening gesture, one she hadn't expected. Involuntarily her gaze lifted, her eyes meeting his. One corner of his mouth quirked up, the movement slight, but enough to tell her that he understood. Which was impossible. An odd pressure suddenly built up in the back of her eyes.

Horrified, she blinked and looked away, clasping her hands together in front of her, and resting them lightly on the table. She drew a quick breath. "John's right. I'll have you and Tom over after Gary and I get settled."

"Really?" Belinda's eyes lit up, then her gaze moved to John. "Kelly and I didn't always get along in school. Although I don't know why. I never cared that she lived with a bunch of hippies."

She turned back to Kelly. "And I didn't say anything ugly about you marrying Gary. I don't know what June Dale told you, but we were all..." Her expression fell and she glanced helplessly at Tom, who was busy trying to unwrap his silverware. Briefly she switched her gaze back to Kelly, then looked down at her hands. "It's just that we were kinda... surprised about the wedding, is all."

Kelly pressed her lips together. Now would be a really good time for Mabel to show up. She twisted around and scanned the room.

"You don't believe me," Belinda said, disappointment lowering her voice.

Kelly sighed. Mabel was nowhere in sight. "I believe you. Can we drop it?"

"I personally think you two make an adorable couple. Honest. You've been friends forever. And it worked out great for Ellie and Ross. But of course everyone could see they were in love," Belinda said thoughtfully. Her eyes widened suddenly. "Not that you and Gary aren't."

The dull ache in Kelly's left temple started throbbing. Why didn't Belinda just shut up? Kelly didn't care about what was being said around town. Nor did she want to hear about it.

And, she realized, she didn't want John to hear it, either.

She slid him a furtive glance. And saw the pity etched in his face.

Damn him.

"Tell you what, Belinda," Kelly said brightly, and reached blindly beneath the table for her briefcase. "You and Tom go ahead and take this booth. John and I have business to discuss and..."

Where the hell was her briefcase? She patted the base of the booth, backhanded the cold metal table pedestal. She swatted the air. Nothing. And then she felt the slightly rough texture of denim. Encasing a leg.

She was groping John.

Jerking her hand back, she started to straighten, but he reached down and grasped her wrist. It was a firm hold and an irrational arrow of fear pierced her scarcely maintained composure.

"I—I'm sorry," she said. "I didn't mean to—"

"Here." His voice was soft, gentle as he pushed the leather briefcase against her palm.

It took her a moment to realize he was trying to help.

"Thank you."

Both their hands were still under the table, their arms swallowed up to their shoulders, their faces indecently close.

"Do you have anything else down here?" he asked, his hazelnut-scented breath stirring the hair near her ear.

Her gaze dropped to his mouth where a tiny speck of sugar rested at the corner. Hit with the sudden and insane urge to lick it off, her breath fluttered in her throat. She swallowed, then tried to form words, but her breathing subsided to a dull rattle in her chest.

He heard the rusty sound. She just knew he did, and her tongue darted out to moisten her lips. His gaze followed the action, then abruptly traveled to her eyes. His eyes turned that midnight blue and told her more than she wanted to know. Her heart skipped three beats.

Belinda cleared her throat.

Kelly looked over the edge of the table at her, and blinked. The woman's eyes were wide with disbelief. *Oh, God.*

Slowly Kelly pulled herself upright. She yanked up the briefcase and set it in full view between John and herself. "I think I have everything," she said calmly, astonished that her voice sounded so normal. "Anyway, as I was saying, since John and I have business to discuss, you two take the table."

When Belinda looked as though she was about to protest, Kelly quickly slid out of the booth, pulling her briefcase along with her.

"Where are you going?" Mabel sped around the lunch counter, holding the coffeepot high in the air as if that was going to keep it from spilling.

Before Kelly could say anything, John levered himself out from behind the table, stood and laid far too much money on the table.

"Hey, you can't do that." Mabel's scowl strung from him to Kelly. "Pick up that money."

Oh, no, Mabel, not now.

It was obvious John didn't know what to do. He reached inside his pocket again. "Sorry, I thought that was enough."

"No way, buster." Mabel picked up the bills and pressed them against John's chest.

The woman had taken him by surprise and he backed into Kelly. Her hand shot out to stop him and ended up cradling the spot where his butt started to curve. He was incredibly firm and it took her a moment to remember she had no business feeling him up this way. She dropped her hand, but the damage had already been done.

The way his midnight gaze swept a path from her face to her chest sent a warm shiver from the back of her neck all the way down to her southern hemisphere.

"No way is Kelly paying a cent in my place," Mabel said, oblivious to the undercurrent.

"Mabel," Kelly drawled in warning.

The older woman jabbed a finger in the air. "Start charging me for all that bookkeeping you do and we'll talk about it.'' She turned her finger on John. "Keep your money."

But he wasn't looking at Mabel. He was looking at Kelly, an odd expression on his face. Then he smiled, leaned over and whispered something in Mabel's ear.

If the entire diner crowd hadn't been craning their necks and ears before, they all but fell out of their seats now. Especially when Mabel, for possibly the first time in her life, shut her mouth, turned three shades of pink and quickly disappeared into the kitchen.

Kelly was pretty speechless herself. She pursed her lips, thought about it for an instant and decided she didn't want to know.

"I think maybe we ought to talk tomorrow," she said to John, and started backing her way toward the door.

She wasn't crazy about leaving him here alone with all these straining ears, but she figured she'd probably cause more harm by sticking around and drooling like a puppy.

Heaven only knew what had come over her. She normally didn't have these kinds of crazy physical reactions. But her palms were starting to get clammy and she swore she could still feel the curve of his buttock pressing against her skin.

"Wait, Kelly." He frowned at her, then glanced uncertainly at the kitchen door.

If he was waiting for Mabel, it was a good chance for Kelly to make a break for it. So when Thelma Perkins waved her over, Kelly did the unthinkable and rudely marched past the woman and her bridge club to the safety of the sidewalk. By the time she fumbled through her purse and found her keys, John appeared at her elbow, a white bag in his hand.

"Didn't you hear me? I asked you to wait." He smiled and held out the bag to her.

Around his broad shoulders, she spotted several faces in the diner's window bobbing above the café curtains. Grudgingly she accepted the bag. "What is it?"

"Apple pie."

That was low. She narrowed her eyes at him, but found no trace of mockery in his expression. A reluctant smile tugged at her mouth. "Thanks."

"My pleasure."

"Well..." She yanked open her car door, forcing him to step back, and felt a surge of relief just having all that metal between them.

He pulled a set of keys out of his pocket. "Where's it going to be?"

"Excuse me?" She squinted at him. From this new angle, a streetlight was shining directly into her eyes and she couldn't see much of his face.

She did, however, see the slow grin curve his mouth when he asked, "Your place or mine?"

Chapter Seven

John followed Kelly down Main Street, past the Save-Rite and Henderson's bakery, and stayed close as she veered off to the left fork in the road. He had a feeling she'd lose him if she could.

She hadn't wanted to invite him to her house. But standing out on Main Street and having half the patrons of Mabel's Diner hanging out the window gawking at her wasn't high on her wish list either. So he'd won by default.

He started to chuckle, then sobered and roughly rammed the gearshift into Third. Had he really won? What the hell was he going to her place for? They had nothing to discuss. The house was going to be completed when it got completed. He shouldn't even be welcoming discussion on the subject. And he sure wasn't using the brains the good Lord gave him by bringing up chemistry. Hadn't he told himself he'd stay out of this mess?

Thanks to a full moon and a handful of stars, the sky wasn't totally black and the old country road was easy to follow without benefit of streetlamps. He had to admit that it had surprised him when she took the left fork leading out of town. Somehow he'd expected her to live on the south side, where a local real-estate company leased some newly built condos.

A lot of things were beginning to surprise him about Kelly. She didn't live in the white house on the hill as he'd thought, for one thing. In fact, it sounded as though she'd lived in a commune. And what was the deal with Mabel? Kelly made her living keeping books, yet she apparently didn't charge for her services. He shook his head. One hour with her and he had more questions than answers.

Not that any of this was his business.

Her taillights disappeared for a moment as her car hugged a curve, and then she turned down a narrow gravel road past a red-white-and-blue mailbox nearly hidden from view by an unruly dogwood branch. He slowed down to put some space between them, then coasted to a stop behind her car, leaving his headlights on while she made her way to the front porch.

He didn't have to wait long. She obviously hadn't locked her door. Quickly she slipped inside and it occurred to him that she may decide to lock it now, leaving him outside. But a second later, soft yellow light flooded the wraparound porch and surrounding shrubs.

He took that as a sign he was still welcome, as begrudging as it may be, and half-smiling, he eased out of the Jeep. When he stepped onto the creaky porch, he saw that she'd left the door slightly ajar, and he knocked twice just to let her know he was entering.

The small dining room to the left caught his attention first. Glass and brass sparkled and shined, and a large Toulouse-Lautrec poster featuring a chorus line hung on the far wall. Directly in front of him was the living room with a suede overstuffed sofa that was far too large for the room. Flanking a chrome-and-glass coffee table sat two black lacquered angular chairs, low to the ground, very modern.

He rubbed the side of his jaw. The inside of Kelly's house looked like a New York apartment. Outside it looked like a farmhouse in desperate need of some fresh paint.

"I'll be right out," she called from somewhere past the dining room. "Do you want coffee or something stronger?"

"Surprise me," he said. She always did.

"Okay, you asked for it."

Grunting, he picked up a piece of pottery and studied the crude design. He'd asked for it, all right. If she brought him coffee, he'd know that she really didn't want him here and he'd go after he finished the one cup. But if she brought him a drink, well, that would tell him something else altogether....

"Ever had a fuzzy navel?"

He turned at the sound of her voice. She set a tray down on the glass coffee table. "Is there a safe answer to that question?" he asked.

She grinned. "I didn't realize how that sounded until I saw the look on your face." With an unsteady hand, she gestured toward the two glasses on the tray. "It's made with orange juice and peach schnapps."

It took him a few moments to realize she was offering him a drink. He was too distracted by the jerky movement of her hand. But his hesitation clearly didn't help to lessen her anxiety because she folded her arms across her chest in a defensive gesture he was beginning to recognize.

She shook back her hair. "If you preferred coffee, you should have said something."

"Nope," he said without hesitation this time, his gaze purposefully meeting hers. "This is exactly what I wanted."

"Fine." Her left foot tapped twice and she glanced off to the right. "Are you going to sit?"

"Sure." Hiding a smile, he returned the small piece of pottery to the foyer table before claiming one of the lacquered chairs. Halfway down, he stopped. This was the damnedest chair he'd ever run across. With its sharp angles and odd construction, the thing nearly defied gravity. He slid another look at the sofa. It was starting to look better by the second.

"Oh, go ahead and try the chair. You'll love it." Kelly set their drinks on coasters and scooted around the table toward the identical chair. "Just sit down like you would any other one," she said, and proceeded to stretch out.

"I don't know...." He frowned. She was a lot smaller than he was. He was going to have a hell of a time getting back up.

"Come on. They're very comfy and good for your posture. I had them specially made."

"I believe it," he mumbled, and eyed the sofa.

"Look, if you're worried about not being able to get up again, I'll help you. But it won't be a problem. Honest."

"Well, if you'll help..."

Apparently she didn't like the way he said that because she gave him an odd look and muttered, "All right, take the couch."

Ignoring her, he gingerly lowered himself onto the contraption. It was impossible to sit upright, yet he wasn't fully reclining either. He felt kind of suspended in limbo. Shifting to the right, he nearly rolled off.

"You didn't design this, did you?" he asked.

"I wish I had. I'd have made a fortune. It's all the rage right now."

"Where? In the land of the Lilliputians?" He tried to center his butt but the entire chair moved instead. Kelly was awfully quiet and he glanced over at her.

Her lips were pressed in a tight line, her chin quivering slightly. Finally she could hold it back no longer and burst out laughing. "This particular design is supposed to accommodate everyone."

"Yeah, well, I'd get my money back if I were you."

With a fair amount of ease, she levered herself from her chair and bent over the drinks. Although her face was averted he knew she was still laughing. When she straightened, she held out his glass. "Fuzzy navel?"

He didn't want to let go of the chair arm. If he did, he was afraid he'd disturb the balance and tip over.

Clearly sensing his unease, she sighed, set down the glass and held out her hand. "You're perfectly safe."

Yeah, but the couch looked safer. He still didn't want to let go of the chair arm. But what was the worst that could happen? He'd roll onto the floor and look like an ass. Or he could break her chair.

Slowly he loosened his grip but kept his elbow firmly anchored. As a test he rocked his body a fraction and nothing crashed. She touched his hand, her warm fingers wrapping around his wrist, her palm pressing against his.

"I've got you," she said, her voice sounding almost hoarse.

He looked into her face. And saw fear.

Her expression startled him and he jerked himself upright, relying on her strength more than he'd planned. She started to fall forward before regaining her footing, then quickly angled her body back as leverage.

But by the time he was out of the chair and standing, he'd dragged her toward him once more and they stood toe to toe, their lips only inches apart.

"Thanks." He searched her upturned face, looking for traces of the anxiety he'd seen earlier.

She blinked, then abruptly withdrew her hand and rubbed her other arm. Stepping back, she said, "Gary never has any problem."

"He likes the chairs?"

She rounded the table, picked up the drinks and handed one to him. "He doesn't say much. He leaves the decorating up to me."

John decided against commenting and moved to the couch.

Returning to the gravity-defying chair, she settled in. Her tongue darted out and she licked the rim of her glass. She made a healthy and thorough sweep before taking a sip. A thoughtful frown puckered her brows. "What do you think?"

Mesmerized by her little ritual, he realized he was staring and quickly brought the glass to his mouth.

Looking both sheepish and wary at the same time, she said, "Moistening the glass keeps the lipstick from clinging."

He nodded, sipped. "A little sweet, but it's not bad."

Her hair had tangled slightly while helping him up and she pushed the mane away from her face. Her hand was shaking again. "I don't drink much...and neither does Gary, so I've been experimenting with different refreshments." After pausing, she added, "To serve at the reception. Gary and I were thinking about making bowls of fuzzy navel punch. So being a little sweet is probably good." She smoothed her skirt. "I thought about tootsie rolls, too. Ever have one of those?" When he arched a brow, she gave him a weak smile and said, "It's another kind of drink. Made with Kahlúa and orange juice."

Her shoulders and chest rose with the deep breath she took as she looked away to glance around the room, her lips absently finding the rim of her glass.

She was chattering, and Kelly was not a chatterer. But he knew what she was doing. He'd heard Gary's name more in the last five minutes than he'd heard her use it during their entire, albeit short, acquaintance.

She sighed. "Of course, champagne punch is always appropriate. Gary thinks so, too."

"I'm surprised you don't have all those details worked out yet. The wedding is...what, three, four weeks away. I figured you'd have everything planned to perfection by now." He thought he was helping her out by contributing to the conversation, but from the annoyed look she gave him, he knew he'd just blown it.

"You sound like Ellie and Lana," she said, gulping down more of her drink. "I've had a lot on my mind, okay?"

He chuckled. "Sure."

"Tax season took up a chunk of my time. I had to help organize the Bachelor Daze festival. Then there was Lana's baby shower, then Ellie's wedding shower, *her* wedding. And then, of course, we had to postpone everything because she eloped. I've been busy."

He shrugged. "Sure."

She scowled at him. "You think my own wedding isn't important to me?"

"I didn't say—"

"I designed most of that house myself. Despite what Bubble—" She waved an impatient hand. "Belinda thinks. I chose the paint, the wallpaper, even the doorknobs and light fixtures. I've already ordered all of the furniture. Heck, I even hand painted the mailbox." She stopped to take a breath.

After a long, awkward pause, he said, "I didn't know we were talking about the house." Which was obviously synonymous with marriage for Kelly.

Her cheeks turned so pink he was sorry he said anything. "That's what you came here to discuss, wasn't it?"

"Yes, ma'am."

"Don't use that tone with me." She did that little shimmy number of hers.

Damn it. He drained his glass.

She settled back and eyed him peevishly. "Do you want another fuzzy navel?"

Trying not to laugh, he shook his head. The last thing she looked like she wanted to do was share another drink with him. Her cheeks were still pink—from irritation, he figured—and her eyes glittered with temper.

"Sorry if I pushed a button," he said as he set his glass on the coaster.

"You didn't."

"My mistake."

"Everyone thinks they're an authority on whether I should get married or not."

"Not me."

She stared at him over the rim of her glass before taking a distracted sip. She licked a stubborn drop from the corner of her mouth and with a hesitant tilt to her head, she asked, "Has Gary ever said anything to you?"

Oh, no. No way was she going to get him to talk. He started to stand but he didn't want to look nervous. He checked out the leather laces on his deck shoes. Both were tied. He massaged the back of his neck. "Like what?"

"About the wedding."

"No."

"About getting married?"

"Look, I don't know the guy that well."

"Two weeks ago he was late coming to dinner because he said he was having a beer with you."

"Yeah, so?" He looked at his watch. "I didn't realize it was so late."

"It's only eight-thirty." Suspicion tainted her voice.

"Yeah, but..." He heard a dog bark in the distance. "I have a date."

She blinked. "Tonight?"

He nodded. "And Goldie hates it when I'm late."

That much was true. In fact, sometimes when she got mad, she peed on the floor to get even, but he figured he'd lose ground by volunteering that information.

"Oh." Surprise and curiosity both paraded across Kelly's face. "Then don't let me keep you."

"Yeah." He inclined his head toward the empty glass. "Thanks for the fuzzy navel."

She nodded and started to stand. But her foot was hooked on the leg of the chair and she teetered briefly before toppling forward.

John jumped over the coffee table and caught her before she could hit the floor. Her hand flailed out and smacked him in a spot that made him grimace, but he cupped her shoulders until she gained her equilibrium.

"I can't believe I did that," she said, looking up at him while unsuccessfully blowing at a strand of hair that fluttered in front of her face.

"Here." He brushed the curl to the side, the back of his fingers trailing the silky texture of her cheek.

"Thanks." She stared up at him, her topaz eyes turning an interesting smoky color, her fingernails still digging lightly into his forearm.

He felt a pull in his groin. Heat swirled in his belly. It was nothing, he told himself—probably aftershocks from the smack she'd given him. Dropping his hand from her shoulder, he shifted slightly away from her. Her fingers slackened on his arm, lingered a moment, then fell away, too.

They were still close, their gazes melting together, but neither of them moved.

The screen door slammed.

"Hey, is that John's Jeep out...?"

They jumped apart. But it was too late.

Gary stood in the doorway, an odd look on his colorless face.

KELLY DISHED UP some Rocky Road ice cream, added a dollop of whipped cream and sprinkled her creation with chopped pecans. She held it up, frowned, then added an extra dollop of whipped cream. Gary really like whipped cream.

She didn't feel guilty, she told herself as she carried the dessert into the living room. She hadn't done anything wrong. Although she had to admit, that hadn't been a pretty scene Gary had walked into fifteen minutes ago. The whole mess had left her uneasy, despite the fact that Gary hadn't seemed bothered and easily accepted their explanation. Plus John's hasty departure hadn't helped. But of course his date was waiting.

"What's the big sigh for?" Gary asked, and she blinked at him in surprise.

She handed him the ice cream, unaware that she had made a sound. "It's been a long day."

"Yeah, for me, too."

She curled up on the couch next to him and put a hand on his thigh. He eyed her hand with ill-concealed interest at first, then dug into the dish of Rocky Road without giving her another glance.

He was probably a little peeved at finding John here. Even if he hadn't said anything. And of course, she didn't generally sit next to him or initiate contact like this.

She sighed again.

He put the spoon down, patted her hand and said, "You want to tell me what's wrong?"

He was looking at her, his kind brown eyes level with hers, reminding her of all the times he'd offered a shoulder when she had been convinced that Sunshine didn't give a rat's behind about her only daughter.

Gary had always been there for her, telling her she was pretty and smart and not to listen to the other kids. She knew she could count on him. Always.

"The house isn't going to be finished on time," she said, and dropped her gaze to her hands. She hadn't lied. So why did she suddenly feel so dishonest?

"Ah." He set the dish on the coffee table, and she looked up in time to see an odd flash of frustration in his eyes. "The weather was touchy this spring."

"I know. I just..." She stared at his familiar face, the way the left corner of his mouth drooped a little lower than the right, the dimple in his left cheek. "Gary, will you kiss me?"

He reared his head back slightly. The movement was subtle but it was also automatic. Disappointment stabbed at her.

"Sure." His eyebrows drawn together in confusion, he leaned forward to brush his lips across hers, then promptly sat back.

She gave him a weak smile. That wasn't exactly what she'd had in mind. "I missed you. I'm glad you came back early."

"Me, too."

She picked at the hem of her skirt. "Could we try that kiss again?"

He smiled, cupped her shoulder with one hand and slid his face closer, pressing his lips firmly to hers.

She kissed him back and waited for that tingly feeling to start. That jittery excitement that she'd felt in high school, anticipating her first kiss. Nothing happened.

Okay, now she felt guilty.

For feeling it earlier.

When John had caught her in his arms.

Sitting back, she took a deep breath and forced a smile for Gary. "Do you want to spend the night? I hate you driving up that winding road with no streetlights."

She knew he wouldn't stay. He never did. And God forgive her, but she didn't want him to.

Sure enough, he shook his head. "I have to get to the office early tomorrow morning. I'm way behind because of tax extensions." He ducked his head to look her in the eyes. "Are you sure you're all right?"

She lifted her chin. "I'm really disappointed about the house is all."

He smiled that infinitely patient smile of his that made his cheek dimple and reminded her what a good, solid, stable husband he was going to make.

"I know, Kelly, but you'll have your house. It just

may take an extra month," he said, rising to his feet. He hesitated, looking down at her, a thoughtful expression on his face. "Do you realize that for months all you've thought about is the house?"

Kelly bit her lip and looked away. She wished that were true. Lately it seemed all she thought about was John Cappel.

Chapter Eight

"Ouch!" Dusty jumped back, away from the strip of molding, letting it dangle over the entry door. "Hell, Cap, you trying to kill me or something?"

The sudden movement startled John and he cut loose a succinct curse. "Hold still."

"Me?" Dusty shook out his hand, then inspected his injured thumb. "You're the one who's gone whacko."

"I barely clipped you."

The younger man shot him a salty look. "This is the third time you clobbered me this week. What's eating you?"

"Nothing. Grab that strip of molding."

"Everything's a damn rush these days," Dusty muttered as he wiped his hand on his jeans, then squinted at his thumb. "This was supposed to be a laid-back, no-hassle job. I feel like I'm back at Fort Ord again."

"That could be arranged."

Dusty laughed. "You wouldn't do that to me. You know how lousy I was at that gig."

John almost smiled at the understatement. ''I know.''

''How about we break for lunch now? My gut's ready to eat my liver.''

''Not until we finish this door,'' he said, wondering where all his patience had gone. He toed the boom box and the static changed to music…a low, bluesy tune that didn't improve his mood.

Dusty was getting on his nerves this week. And John was sick of Goldie's spiteful attempts to get his attention. The dog was totally undisciplined and an all-around royal pain. Tonight she was going to get only half a steak.

''Oh-oh.'' Dusty's voice lowered and he used his eyes to indicate a spot behind John. ''The enemy's approaching at twenty-three hundred.''

As soon as John glanced over his shoulder, he saw Kelly step through the back door, then stop to survey the kitchen.

Her dress was an inch shorter than what Bachelor Falls probably considered decent and he muttered another curse when his entire body reacted in agreement.

''Go get lunch,'' he said to Dusty.

''You just said—''

''If you want lunch, beat it.''

Scowling, Dusty hit the side of his jeans and dust filtered throughout the sunlit air, settling on the metal toolbox sitting near his feet. He frowned, and slapped his leg again. More dust. Then he smelled the armpit of his shirt and made a face.

''Ah, Cap, I think I need to come over and use your washer again tonight.''

"Fine." John started spreading out his tools, shuffling stacks of molding, trying to look busy. He wasn't ready to see her yet. Especially after the visit Gary had paid him three days ago.

Pursing his lips, Dusty watched with blatant curiosity. "You want I should pick you up some lunch? Your fridge was mighty bare last time I looked."

"Stay out of my refrigerator and it won't bother you."

Dusty's eyebrows shot together. "Well, excuse the hell out of me."

"Hey, I'll tell you what you can do for me." John dug into his pocket. Dusty was right. John had purposely stayed away from town to the point that all he had left in the refrigerator was a steak, one tomato and a bottle of ketchup. "After lunch pick up some groceries, take them to the cabin, then you can do your laundry while you're still on the clock. It's on me." He passed the younger man some money. "Deal?"

Dusty pocketed the bills and grinned. "Hell, yeah. Does that mean I'm done for the day?"

John thought for a moment. "I'll leave that up to you."

His friend's smile faded. "You know I hate it when you pull that fatherly crap." His gaze strayed toward Kelly. She'd left the kitchen and was inspecting the dining room. A slow grin returned to Dusty's mouth and he gave John a teasing look. "I think I'll probably mosey on back here and check things out."

"Suit yourself." *Bloody hell.* The last thing John or Kelly needed was idle speculation. He picked up his hammer and ignored Dusty until the younger man finally ambled toward the door.

"Let Goldie out while you're there," John called out and Dusty waved acknowledgment right before he disappeared outside.

When John turned around, he found Kelly standing several feet away.

She was giving him a funny, slightly hostile look. After letting a brief silence fester, she arched a brow and asked, "Is Goldie a dog?"

He instantly recalled their conversation that night at her house. *Damn.* "She doesn't think so," he said, and presented her with his back as he crouched down to poke through his toolbox.

"Hmm, I would never have guessed you to be such a chicken."

Smiling to himself, he ignored the bait and continued to occupy himself with his tools. It wasn't his fault she'd assumed Goldie was his date. Okay, so maybe it was.

"Have you talked to Gary recently?" she asked hesitantly, and he didn't have to look up to picture her doing that shimmy number.

Oh, man. He rubbed the sudden warning itch at the back of his neck. "Why?"

"He had to leave town again and he wants me to keep tabs on the house."

She stepped around the toolbox to get his attention and when he lifted his gaze all he saw were two silky, lightly tanned thighs. A pair of freckles sat two inches above her left knee and a tiny scar paralleled the hem of her short skirt.

"Did you hear me?"

He inhaled deeply and faced down again. "I heard you."

Silence.

"Gary said we might not have enough molding for the guardrail in the dining room." She shuffled her sandaled feet, then shifted her weight from one foot to the other.

He was tempted to look up and see where the freckles had landed, instead his gaze strayed to her toenails. They were tinted a soft pink. And looked sexy as hell.

He stood suddenly. "I have a lot of work to do. Is there something in particular you wanted?"

"What's wrong? Is there another snafu with the house?" At his perplexed frown, she made a small uncertain movement with one shoulder. "I can hear your accent when you're angry or upset."

Bloody hell. The unpredictable accent bugged him, and that she could so easily read him irritated him even more.

"Nothing is wrong," he said, reaching for the volume button on the radio. "You don't have to keep showing up here. I know how to do my job."

She stooped suddenly, her hand shooting out to cover his. "Don't do that." Her hold slackened when his eyes abruptly met hers. "Please."

His fingers broke contact with the switch. "Okay."

Her hand lingered across his. "I didn't—" Her gaze searched his face for a moment before she lowered it to her toes. "I promise not to keep you long."

Her soft touch made his skin itch with desire and he pulled away to reach into his pocket for some nails. She jerked back, too, as if he'd stung her.

Distress shadowed her eyes as she stared at him and he knew it had nothing to do with insufficient molding or when the house would be finished.

"Okay," he said, laying down the hammer and slowly straightening. "You have my undivided attention. What can I do for you?"

She blinked. As her gaze settled at a point somewhere on his chest, a faint pink started at her neck. He would have given up his entire prized collection of Beatles albums to know what she was thinking.

"Tell me about the molding," she said, turning away to study the far wall. "Is there more on order?"

The back of her skirt was creased from sitting and there were marks across her legs from the car seat. One side of the fabric was particularly crinkled, making the skirt hike up. He could see that the crisscross pattern traveled way up her thigh.

He wondered what color underwear she was wearing.

The thought came out of left field, shocking him.

He had never once speculated on what sort of underwear a woman was wearing before. And certainly not an engaged woman. This had to stop.

She lifted on tiptoes to study the molding over the study door.

No panty lines.

He'd bet it was one of those thongs. Pink or peach. With a little lace.

"I don't remember if—" She turned suddenly to face him, and it was too late for him to pretend he wasn't looking at her rear end. She automatically tugged at the hem of her skirt.

Nonchalantly he'd raised his gaze to level his eyes with hers. "Remember what?"

"Is there something on my skirt?" She twisted around and pulled at the back of the skirt to have a look, causing the front to ride up so high he thought his heart would give out.

"There's nothing on your skirt."

His tone was sharp and she turned accusing eyes on him. "Then what were you looking at?" As if she didn't believe him, she reached around for another look.

He passed a hand down his face. "I was wondering what kind of underwear you have on."

She froze. Then she spun back toward him. "What did you say?"

"Want to put me out of my misery and enlighten me?"

Incredulous, she stared at him. "You're serious."

"Don't play dumb. You knew where I was looking. You decided to call me on it. Now you wanna penalize me for being honest. Fine." He snatched up his hammer, his annoyance more self-directed than anything else.

"No, I mean you were really looking *there*."

At the strange tone of her voice, his gaze drew back to her and he glimpsed shock melting into delight. The rapt expression lasted a mere second or two, and then a mask of outrage took its place.

She placed her hands on her hips. "You're trying to distract me from talking about the house again, but it's not going to work."

Pursing his lips, he indulged a sudden suspicion by raking a slow gaze down the length of her body. Her pale yellow blouse was a snug fit across her breasts, the fabric disappearing into the narrow waistband of her linen skirt. Her hips flared perfectly, and under his scrutiny, he noticed her hands slacken and slide a fraction along the curve.

Her feet shifted nervously, her pink-tipped toes curling toward the concrete floor.

"It's not working," she said, but her voice was breathless, her posture uncertain.

And he knew that she hadn't been faking. There was no question the attention both surprised and pleased her. She didn't know how desirable she really was.

As much as John liked Gary, he knew the guy was an idiot. A spineless idiot who not only couldn't admit to Kelly that he didn't want to marry her, but had left a nick in her confidence.

"Are you finished?" she asked, and he looked up to see her crossing her arms.

He thought in silence for a moment, then said, "Okay, you want to talk? We can do it after work. Right now, you're slowing me down."

"We tried that," she said dryly.

"We'll stay away from Mabel's or Hazel's. In fact, come by my place around seven-thirty. That makes more sense."

"Why?"

"Because not even the mailman makes it that far up the hill. Other than Dusty I've never seen another soul past Old Man Feeney's barn. No one will know you're there."

"I don't care if—"

"Kelly, cut the bull. You do care."

"You're wrong." She shook her head. "Well, not totally. I don't care about the gossip. But it bothers Gary. And I do care about that."

He studied her for a moment. Was this what this marriage was about? Saving face? "So, you want to meet at my place?"

"Why can't we talk here?"

"We can." He shrugged. "But there's beer and steaks at my house." At least he hoped there were. Dusty wasn't always reliable.

A small reluctant smile tugged at her lips. "Won't that upset your date?"

"Not if you pat her tummy and give her bites."

She laughed, then worried her lower lip. "It's not like we have a lot to discuss. I just wanted to check on the molding and see if the entry door arrived yet and—"

"And we can do all of that tonight."

"Well, it seems silly to—"

A car door slammed, and then another. The men were back from lunch.

Her gaze darted toward the sound and her hand fluttered in a nervous gesture as she tucked a strand of hair behind her ear. "See, the thing is—"

"Look, Kelly..." He smiled reassuringly. "I know you want to discuss the house and I promise you that's exactly what we'll do."

She lifted her shoulder in a tiny shrug and a strange expression crossed her face. "Actually, I wanted to talk about chemistry."

"I'VE GOT TO TELL YOU, Kelly, I'm really proud of you for not butting into this shower," Ellie said as she calculated the final guest total. "I didn't think you could do it but I haven't heard a word out of you about it in over a week."

Lana grinned, her hand absently rubbing her swollen belly. "Amazing, isn't it? What's the final count?"

"Everyone is coming. Mabel said she might be a little late. But she's closing the diner early and doesn't expect to be much past eight."

Kelly watched her two friends pore over the numerous lists they'd made. She wanted to get excited about the shower. She really did. They had worked hard on planning every last detail despite their own busy lives with their new husbands. But the excitement wouldn't come.

"Kelly? Are you listening?" Lana leaned across the kitchen table and touched her arm.

"What?"

Her friends exchanged worried glances. "Your house will be just fine," Lana said. "What difference will a few weeks make?"

Kelly sighed. Worrying about the house had been simple. Wishing Gary looked at her the way John did wasn't. She looked thoughtfully at Ellie. "When did you know for sure Ross was the one?"

Ellie blinked in surprise, her gaze sliding to Lana, who frowned, her hand stilling on her belly.

"I mean, you knew him all your life and suddenly one day you had to say, wow, this guy really knocks my socks off." Kelly watched uneasily as her friends both started to smile. She shouldn't have brought this up. An open can of worms was not what she needed right now.

"You're not the first person to get cold feet, Kelly," Lana said, turning to get a glass of water.

Ellie laughed. "Half the guys in this town have feet so cold they're blue."

"Did you?" Kelly asked. "Did you get cold feet?"

Ellie sobered. "My circumstances were different."

"What about you, Lana?"

The glass halfway to her lips, Lana's hand froze and she returned to the table, her eyes not quite meeting Kelly's. "You have to admit, mine was not the usual courtship, either."

Kelly stared down at the piece of paper she'd been shredding.

"Have you tried on your dress recently?" Lana asked brightly. "You look like you might have lost a few pounds in the past week. I bet it'll fit better now."

"Yeah." Ellie lifted her baseball cap and smoothed back her hair before resettling the cap on her head. "Go try it on."

Kelly shook her head. She had lost some weight and the dress would probably fit better. She just wasn't interested right now. "Maybe later."

"You can't later," Lana said. "We have to go to Clarksville and talk to the caterer. You haven't forgotten, have you?"

Kelly straightened. "That's tonight?"

"Sure. We made the appointment last week, remember?"

"Right."

Lana and Ellie looked at each other. "I think it's too late to cancel," Lana said. "Did something come up?"

Kelly propped her elbow on the table and let her chin sink into her palm. This was just as well. She had no business going to John's place tonight. She'd known the moment she agreed to go that it was wrong.

Especially when he looked at her the way he did. Especially when it sent a hot thrill straight from the crown of her head to the tips of her toes. It wasn't right. Gary should be the one looking at her like he wanted to devour her with his eyes.

But Gary had never looked at her like that before. Never. No one had.

"I suppose Lana and I could go alone," Ellie said when Kelly didn't answer. "But we figured you'd want final say."

"No," Kelly said quickly. "I want to go. What time are we leaving?"

"About an hour okay with you?"

"Fine." She rose from the table, wondering if John was listed with directory assistance. He hadn't lived there long enough to be in the phone book. "I have to take care of a couple of things before we leave."

"Me, too." Ellie grabbed her keys off the table, and Lana stood, too. "Shall we meet back here in an hour?"

"Sounds like a plan," Kelly said absently.

This was a perfect way out of meeting John. She did have a lot to discuss with him, but she wasn't sure now was the right time. She was feeling a little too vulnerable and she didn't like making decisions or doing anything while in such an emotional state.

Her gaze snagged on her friends. They were silently watching her, concern etched in their faces. She wanted to tell them about John and the new and strange feelings he'd provoked inside her. They were her very best friends and wouldn't think of judging her, and it would feel good to unload. But she was too ashamed. Ashamed to be having traitorous thoughts when Gary had been so kind and supportive all her life.

Besides, what was there to really tell them? She was going to marry Gary. There was no question about that. He was solid and stable and loyal. He'd make the perfect husband.

Even if he didn't look at her as if she were a chocolate parfait on a hot summer's day.

Sighing, she walked them to the door and waited until they got in Ellie's car before she picked up the phone. She wasn't surprised to find that John wasn't listed. Somehow she didn't think he even had a phone. Probably didn't have an alarm clock, either, she decided as she hopped in her car and headed up the hill toward his house. It wouldn't suit his foot-loose life-style.

She glanced at her watch. She had just enough time to tell him she wouldn't be there for dinner after all. It would be a quick visit. Not even a visit. She'd just run in and out. No discussion about chemistry, or even the house. From now on she was staying away. Gary could handle everything as soon as he returned at the end of the week.

Yup.

She took a deep breath as she turned up his driveway. Everything would revert to normal. They had nothing more to say to each other.

Rounding the final bend, her foot quickly switched

from the accelerator to the brake as she stared in surprise.

What the hell was Gary's distinctive bronze Saturn doing parked in front of John's cabin?

Chapter Nine

John pulled his Jeep alongside Kelly's compact, turned off the engine and sat with his wrist draped over the wheel, his hand dangling as he stared at her house. Two lamps lit up the living room, while another glowed through the curtains at the far right of the house.

He could turn around and go home, and she probably wouldn't even know he'd come. Seeing her car and knowing she was home safe was enough, wasn't it? At least now he could get a decent night's sleep instead of worrying that she'd wrapped herself around a tree trying to navigate the poorly lit, winding road he lived on.

Shaking his head, he heaved a weary sigh. Normally he didn't waste time worrying, but for the last couple of hours he could think of little else other than why Kelly hadn't shown up for dinner. It wasn't like her to chump him like that. From everything he'd seen and heard, she was punctual and dependable. Something had to have happened. And there was only one way to find out what that was.

He swung out of the Jeep, leaving the keys in the

ignition, and headed down the stone path toward her porch. He kicked a pebble out of the way, then slowed down when he realized his temper had started to flare.

She had a lot of nerve standing him up the way she had, without even a phone call, as if his time wasn't as valuable as hers.

Bloody hell.

He took the first step and reminded himself to give her a chance to explain. They weren't going to get anywhere if he jumped down her throat.

The front wood-paneled door was open, leaving only the screen door to keep out two fluttering moths trying to get to the dimly lit lamp just inside the entryway.

Another pair of lights flickered deeper in the living room. About to knock, John hesitated when he realized it came from two candles sitting atop the mantel.

And then he saw her.

Sitting in profile, she stared pensively at a piece of canvas, an artist's paintbrush in her left hand. She wore a large white T-shirt over white leggings, both liberally smudged with pinks and blues and oranges, and her hair was pulled back in a lopsided ponytail.

She swiped some red onto her brush and dabbed the color onto the canvas. Angling her head, she made a face at the result.

He smiled. Always the perfectionist.

Tendrils of hair spiraled across her cheek and she blew at the wisps distractedly, her concentration fully on her work.

He wanted to see what she was painting. Her hobby surprised him. He'd have guessed her too impatient.

But he was discovering there was a lot about her he didn't know. Not that any of it should interest him.

And that was a large part of his problem. He was interested all right. And he'd bet his pension she was, too.

He watched for another couple of minutes as she made broad strokes with her brush. The more she wielded it, the more relaxed she seemed to become. She stopped to take a sip of what looked like tea and smiled at her creation.

Slowly, without a sound, he leaned to the right. From this new angle he caught a glimpse of the watercolor and a slow sad smile curved his lips. Kelly was going to have to stick to keeping books for a living. She was no Picasso. But he was certain that didn't matter to her. In the middle of a field of wildflowers sat her house, white picket fence and all.

He knew he had to leave then. Without saying a word to her. She was safe. That was the important thing. There was nothing for him to say tonight. Or the next day, for that matter.

All Kelly wanted was her house and a nice predictable life in Bachelor Falls. She'd be happy.

That should be enough for him, too. Somehow it wasn't.

Quietly he turned and left.

"I DON'T THINK we've forgotten anything." Lana wrinkled her nose, her hand resting, as it often did, on her belly. "Kelly, you shouldn't even be here until the shower starts. Isn't it bad luck or something?"

Kelly chewed at her new manicure. "I don't understand how you could have misplaced Purple Bunny, Ellie. He needs to be here.''

"Okay, tar and feather me if it'll make you feel better." The ever-practical Ellie was a quart low on patience today—thanks to Kelly, who was making everyone nuts. "Just wait until after this shower is over, all right?" Frowning, Ellie scanned the buffet table. "Lana, did anyone pick up the cake?"

"I did," Hazel yelled from across the hall. "Serena is bringing it in from the car."

Kelly stared sheepishly at her hot pink fingernails. She'd been a pain in the rear all week. It's a wonder her friends were still talking to her at all.

Knowing full well what the problem was, she should've had the gumption to take care of it days ago. But, no...ever since the night she'd failed to show up at John's place for dinner, she'd studiously avoided the construction site or anyplace else she thought she might run into him. The whole thing was truly amazing. She had no idea she had it in her to be such a wimp.

"Is Gary coming to this shindig?" Melva asked as she passed Kelly with an armload of brightly wrapped presents.

"No." Kelly looked up. "No men allowed at this one," she said, and glimpsed Tommie Nell snickering behind a large bouquet of freshly cut wildflowers, her mischievous gaze darting toward Melva.

Oh, hell. She hoped her fiancé wasn't going to show up as a surprise. She hadn't talked to Gary since spotting his car at John's several nights ago. Although he'd called once, he'd gotten her answering machine.

Which was just as well, since she wasn't ready to talk to him yet.

Worried, she grabbed Ellie by the shirtsleeve and dragged her off to the side. "Gary isn't coming, is he?"

"Not that I know of. Isn't he still out of town?"

"Yeah, I think so." A sudden depression fogged Kelly. She didn't want to think that Gary had purposely misled her. But he'd distinctly told her he'd be leaving town that morning. By the time she's seen his car at John's place, Gary should have been on the other side of the state.

She hoped the misunderstanding meant there was a surprise in her future. He could've gone to see John because he was doing something extra in the house, she'd told herself. Or maybe he'd found the paneled doors she'd originally wanted. Maybe the two of them had figured a way to get the house completed on time.

But none of those things were consistent with Gary's character. Spontaneity wasn't in his vocabulary, and heaven forbid that he'd do anything without checking with her first.

No, she had a bad feeling about his visit to John's. His message on her machine two days later indicated that he was still working with a client six hours away and wouldn't be arriving home until tonight. He'd said nothing about leaving town late. If she didn't know better, she'd think he was cheating on her. Which was a totally ludicrous idea.

"What's the matter?" Ellie frowned. "You look bad."

"Gee, thanks."

"You're not on one of those crazy grapefruit diets again, are you?

Kelly shook her head. "I haven't even been able to think about food lately."

Ellie's eyes widened in alarm. "This is more serious than I thought." At Kelly's dirty look, her friend grinned. "Relax. I promise we've thought of every last detail. This shower is going to be perfect."

"Except Purple Bunny isn't here."

Ellie squinted, her frustration saturating the air around them. "If you're trying to make me feel guilty, you've done an excellent job. But unfortunately, I still don't know where he is."

Kelly leaned forward and hugged her friend. "I'm sorry. I don't want you to feel guilty. Honest, I don't. I just..."

She let her voice trail off because she couldn't trust it. Emotion welled all the way up to her throat. Ellie had looked so beautiful and happy at her wedding. So had Lana. It had been clear both their husbands, Ross and Blake, were crazy in love with their wives.

And Kelly had suddenly felt the ugly sting of jealousy. She desperately wanted Gary to look at her the way Blake looked at Lana, the way Ross looked at Ellie.

The way John had looked at her.

Too bad John was the wrong man.

"Hey." Ellie pulled back from the embrace and tried to look Kelly in the eyes. "Something *is* wrong."

Kelly glanced away, across the room to where Tommie Nell and Hazel were arguing over where the two bouquets of helium balloons should go. The town hall looked nice. Everyone had pitched in to decorate it. The least Kelly could do was try her best to have a good time.

Ellie touched her arm and Kelly snapped out of her self-absorbed fog and forced a smile. "Just getting a little sentimental, I guess."

"I know. And I bet Purple Bunny shows up in time for the wedding." Ellie's sad smile perked up. "Hey, maybe he's at my mom's house. Or with Auntie Om. Have you asked her? She and my mom carted off all the wedding presents after Ross and I ducked out of the reception."

Kelly shook her head. "She knows I'm looking for him. She would have said something."

Bumped from behind, Kelly turned around to find Melva and Ida Whipple dragging a table across the floor. Ida held up a hand for Melva to stop, then fanned herself while she caught her breath.

Melva eyed the two younger women. "Would you two quit your yakking and get a move on? We want everything ready before the entertainment starts."

"Entertainment?" Kelly frowned at Ellie, who shrugged.

"Entertainment?" Hazel echoed from across the room, and two other women groaned. She pushed the balloons aside and scowled at Tommie Nell. "If you think we're listening to Jimmy play that dang banjo of his—"

"Oh, quiet." Tommie Nell promptly rearranged the balloons to her liking. "He's not playing the banjo. We're going to have—" She cut herself short and flashed a mischievous grin at her audience. "A surprise."

Oh, great. This was just great. For two cents, Kelly would crawl back into bed, headfirst, under the covers. If Tommie Nell was in charge of entertainment, no telling what to expect. Ellie and Lana knew better. What had they been thinking?

Kelly squinted at her friend. "Look, Eliot..."

Ellie bristled. "Don't Eliot me. I had nothing to do with this."

Both women automatically looked at Lana, who was several feet away, licking chocolate frosting off the fingers of one hand.

Kelly and Ellie grinned and looked at each other at the same time. In unison, they said, "Nah."

Ellie laughed. "She hasn't had time to worry about entertainment. She's been too busy chasing chocolate or smooching with Blake."

Emotion clogged Kelly's throat and it was a struggle to keep a smile in place. She and Gary never smooched. Pecked on the cheek was more like it. She shook away the thought. It would depress her and she couldn't afford that. Not today when everyone had gone to so much trouble.

"Here, let's help them move this table," she said, stepping toward Ida and Melva.

The two older women gladly relinquished their task with only a mild scolding that Kelly wasn't even supposed to be here yet. Kelly laughed at their remarks, then helped Ellie put the table in place.

For the next fifteen minutes she busied herself with the decorations while quietly listening to all the chatter and gossip.

By six-thirty, streams of pink and white crepe paper looped from the ceiling, and balloons bobbed in riotous colors throughout the room. They had to add a small chest at the end of the buffet table to accommodate all the food.

For convenience's sake, Ellie and Lana had insisted on the shower being catered. The older set hadn't liked that decision one bit, but after everyone got over their grumbling about the errant ways of the new generation, they all oohed and aahed over the mouthwatering assortment of color-coordinated appetizers, pasta salads and cold chicken dishes.

Then Hazel found out that Mabel had contributed four of her prizewinning apple pies on the sly, and for ten minutes stuff pretty much hit the fan. Spitting nails, Hazel ran to the Hash House and hauled back five dozen homemade chocolate chip cookies and added three slabs of the day's leftover meat loaf. People from three counties often came to Bachelor Falls just for that particular award-winning dish, and Hazel lifted her chin in smug satisfaction when the three mangled pieces were the first to disappear.

Biting back a grin, Kelly dug into her pasta salad, and whispered to Lana, "I should have eloped like Ellie."

"It wouldn't matter. They would've given you a shower when you got back, too."

Kelly nodded, laughing. At the insistence of everyone, she'd been first through the buffet line. Lana's pregnancy had earned her the second position, and now they sat together in the corner, eating, watching the parade of older women poke critically at the spread of dishes, clucking their tongues at the extravagant use of garnishes.

Everything apparently passed muster, however, because it didn't take long for most of the food to disappear. Even Ona Mae ate without creating a scene and pointing out every unhealthy ingredient on the menu. Still, most of the women made sure they got to the food before Ona Mae could pull out anything she found objectionable.

Melva didn't waste a minute getting the table cleared. "Hurry up and eat, everyone," she said as she started filling large trash bags. "So we can start playing games."

The older women smiled. The younger ones groaned.

"I thought the entertainment was supposed to be here already?" Mabel grumbled. She was still miffed with Hazel. Once set in motion, their tiffs generally lasted a couple of days.

"Any minute," Tommie Nell said cheerfully and glanced at the door.

Everyone else looked, too, their wary gazes sending signals of misgiving. Sometimes Tommie Nell had an odd sense of humor. Many of the women figured it was because she'd been a widow too long and they blamed her beau, Jimmy Bartlett, for her shortcomings.

"Do you swear you don't know what this surprise entertainment is about?" Kelly's gaze followed the direction of Lana's grin, and she caught Tommie Nell's blatantly furtive attempt to tiptoe out the door.

"Not a clue. Honest."

The words were barely out of Lana's mouth when Tommie Nell came charging back into the hall, her hands waving wildly. "Get ready, girls," she said, and reached under a chair in the corner.

Play the

"LAS VEGAS"

GAME

GET
**3 FREE
GIFTS!**

FREE
GIFTS!

FREE
GIFTS!

FREE
GIFTS!

TURN THE PAGE TO PLAY! Details
inside!

Play the
"LAS VEGAS
and get
3 FREE GIFTS

FREE GIFTS!

1. Pull back all 3 tabs on the card at right. Then check the cla
   see what we have for you — 2 FREE BOOKS and a gift—ALL
   FREE!

2. Send back this card and you'll receive brand-new Harlequin
   Romance® novels. These books have a cover price of $3.99
   are yours to keep absolutely free.

3. There's no catch. You're under no obligation to buy anything
   nothing — ZERO — for your first shipment. And you don't
   any minimum number of purchases — not even one!

4. The fact is thousands of readers enjoy receiving books by ma
   Harlequin Reader Service™. They like the convenience of hor
   they like getting the best new novels BEFORE they're available
   and they love our discount prices!

5. We hope that after receiving your free books you'll want to re
   subscriber. But the choice is yours — to continue or cancel, a
   all! So why not take us up on our invitation, with no risk of any
   You'll be glad you did! *Yours Free!*

Play the

"LAS VEGAS" Game

YES! I have pulled back the 3 tabs. Please send me all the free Harlequin American Romance® books and the gift for which I qualify. I understand that I am under no obligation to purchase any books, as explained on the back and opposite page.

(U-H-AR-06/98)   **154 HDL CF7Y**

NAME _____ (PLEASE PRINT CLEARLY) _____

ADDRESS _____ APT. _____

CITY _____ STATE _____ ZIP _____

GET 2 FREE BOOKS & A FREE MYSTERY GIFT!

GET 2 FREE BOOKS!

GET 1 FREE BOOK!

TRY AGAIN!

Offer limited to one per household and not valid to current Harlequin American Romance® subscribers. All orders subject to approval.

PRINTED IN U.S.A.

BUSINESS REPLY MAIL

FIRST-CLASS MAIL   PERMIT NO. 717   BUFFALO NY

POSTAGE WILL BE PAID BY ADDRESSEE

HARLEQUIN READER SERVICE
3010 WALDEN AVE
PO BOX 1867
BUFFALO NY 14240-9952

NO POSTAGE
NECESSARY
IF MAILED
IN THE
UNITED STATES

She pulled out something long and black and Kelly had to duck her head around Lana to see it. About the same time she realized it was a boom box, Tommie Nell flipped a switch and loud rock music crashed the party. Ida Whipple nearly fell out of her seat, and Ona Mae threw up her hands in disgust. Everyone else winced and clamped hands over their ears.

Tommie Nell made an adjustment to the volume, then straightened and stared expectantly at the door. Kelly followed her gaze.

Five seconds later, John stepped into the room.

Wearing his usual work clothes—faded jeans and well-washed T-shirt clinging to every contour of his chest—he stopped in the doorway. The frame was narrow and his broad shoulders filled a good portion of the space. He shoved a hand through his dark windblown hair, streaked with gold from the sun, his puzzled gaze bouncing from one openmouthed face to the next.

Slowly, one by one, the few women who had their backs to him started turning around and staring, too.

Kelly's heart somersaulted down to her stomach. The loud music made her slightly nauseous. What the hell was he doing here?

Tommie Nell started to clap. No one heard her at first, so she turned down the volume again, then grinning broadly, still clapping, she yelled, "Take it off."

Melva's eyes widened to the size of Mabel's apple pies, and Ida Whipple looked a little pale. But everyone else got past their stunned looks and started putting their hands together, too.

"Come on, girls." Tommie Nell stopped clapping long enough to rouse everyone with a few enthusiastic waves, then went back to chanting, "Take it off! Take it off!"

Ida clucked her disapproval, pushed her wide hips off the chair and waddled toward the rest room in a huff. No one but Kelly and a gaping Lana seemed to notice. All eyes were on John.

Within seconds, three women joined Tommie Nell's chant. A moment later, two more added their voices to the choir.

Then one lone, shrill enthusiast was heard above the rest. "Take it *all* off!"

The look on John's face was priceless, and Kelly would have really enjoyed it if she weren't so shocked herself. He backed up a step, his gaze darting around the room as if he thought everyone had gone crazy. Which they had.

"Is he taking everything off?" Melva murmured in nonplussed disbelief.

"What?" Her gaze glued to John, Hazel batted blindly beneath her chair until she found her purse. "What's he taking off?" she asked, pushing a pair of sixties glasses up the bridge of her nose.

"Well, it ain't a few pounds," Mabel said, snickering and nudging her former foe with her elbow. "He's damn near perfect."

Letting out a huff of exasperation, Lana leaned toward Kelly. "I got in trouble for saying damn in her diner once."

"What are you waiting for?" Tommie Nell bellowed, leaping from her chair. "Take *something* off."

Melva leaned over and whispered, "We gotta get that girl married if we have to drag Jimmy out of the falls ourselves."

Kelly shook her head. Was John moonlighting? Didn't he make enough money as a carpenter? She couldn't believe he'd agreed to do this, although he seemed to be panicking now. It served him right.

"Ladies, please." He held up his hands, palms out.

"What's the matter, lover? Need a volunteer?" Tommie Nell reached him in record time and a second before the crowd's collective gasp, she yanked at his belt buckle and pulled.

Chapter Ten

John jumped back, fisting a handful of leather at the
same time. He'd been a hair away from losing his
belt to the short plump blonde. The woman was nuts.

He sent a wary glance around the room. They all
were. The average age had to be in the upper forties
and yet they'd all been hooting and hollering like a
bunch of wild animals. Were these women raised by
wolves?

"Are we rushing you, honey?" The blonde smiled
and held out her hand. "I'll hold anything you want
to start with."

Certain he had a firm grip on his belt, he backed
up, feeling a trail of perspiration form along the base
of his neck. "I don't know what you're talking about,
lady. I came here to give an estimate."

The blonde laughed. "I spoiled things, didn't I?
You probably wanted to do a little skit first or something."

"Quit hogging him, Tommie Nell," Mabel hollered over the waning chants. "We can't hear."

"Hell with that. I can't see." Hazel angled her

head to the side, while stretching her neck. "Move that big rear end of yours, Tommie."

The blonde threw a quelling look over her shoulder.

No one paid much attention to the exchange. All eyes were still on him.

All right. He was out of here. No more being polite. No more Mr. Nice Guy. He was simply getting the hell out of here. No matter what it took. And never, he promised himself, never would he so much as look at a woman twice again. This was bloody humiliating.

Just as he was about to bolt for the door, he saw her.

Kelly was huddled in the corner next to another woman about her age. He stopped, almost as stunned at suddenly seeing her as he'd been when the chanting had started. He didn't know how he'd missed her earlier, except that he'd totally lost it when he realized what these women had expected.

What the hell did she have to do with all of this?

The woman Mabel had referred to as Tommie Nell sidled up to him, frowning, and latched onto his arm. "You're not thinking of leaving, are you? I paid for a full half hour."

"I have no idea what you're talking about," he said, extricating his arm from her hold. Looking over her head, he crooked a finger at Kelly. "Could I see you for a moment?"

Everyone turned to see who he was talking to. Kelly had scrunched down so that only her eyes and the top of her head showed, but she lifted her chin and stood when everyone waited to see what she would do.

"How does she know him?" the older woman with the tall, stiff hairdo loudly asked her neighbor.

"He's that carpenter working on her place."

"Ohh."

"I heard about him," someone else said.

A lot of low murmuring echoed throughout the room, but John ignored it and waited for Kelly to weave her way out of the thicket of curious faces all aimed at him. When he was fairly certain she wasn't going to bolt in the opposite direction, he backed into the hall away from the prying stares, and waited.

As soon as she rounded the corner, he saw the anger in her eyes. Anger he didn't understand. He was the one who these woman had just made a bloody fool of.

She stopped several feet in front of him, folded her arms across her chest and gave him the silent treatment.

With great effort, John unclenched his teeth. "What's going on here?"

"Good question."

"Yeah, and I'd like the answer."

Her brows drew slightly together and she looked disappointed. "Doesn't Gary pay you enough?"

"Meaning?"

"I thought carpenters made decent salaries. Apparently I was wrong. You ought to look into a more stable profession. One that doesn't require you to moonlight as a stripper."

"What?" Every bone in his body went on the defensive. He didn't know what ticked him off more, that she thought he was here to strip for a bunch of depraved women, or that his being a carpenter wasn't good enough for Miss High-and-Mighty. "You think I should be an accountant?"

"You say it like it's a dirty word." She snorted. "I can't believe your gall."

"I make more money in one day than an accountant makes in three." He'd almost said Gary. But this wasn't about her fiancé, or even about money.

Her chin lifted higher. "Maybe. *When* you can get work. But you can't always count on that, can you?"

"I can count on myself."

"Stripping?"

Shaking his head, he stared at her. "I'm sorry for you."

"Me?" Anger made her topaz eyes flash with gold fire. "I'm not the one degrading myself for a few bucks because I can't stay in one place long enough to hold down a decent job."

"You have all the answers, don't you?" Slowly he burrowed his hands into his pockets. "Everything nice and safe in your predictable little world." He half smiled and took another step back. "See you around, Kelly."

She uncrossed her arms, and he saw her fists clench as they dropped to her sides. "Aren't you going to give them their money's worth?"

He ignored the taunt. He'd hurt her. His psyche wasn't in such great shape either. He was ashamed he'd made the remark about accountants and money. That was petty. But she'd pushed a button. Because at one time he did care. Sometimes he still had to struggle against getting sucked back into believing his identity was tied to other people's opinions, the amount that appeared on his check or the number of stripes on his sleeve.

The thought disgusted him and he shook his head and turned on his heel. He had a fleeting glimpse of Kelly's pale, disbelieving face as he headed toward the door. Before he got there, Tommie Nell came barreling down the hall.

"Wait a minute," she said. "Shorty promised you'd give us a full half hour. You haven't even taken anything off yet."

Shorty? What the hell was this about? John slowed down. He could leave and ignore her or he could turn around and straighten this out once and for all. He stopped, sighing with disgust, and turned.

Before he could utter a sound, he heard the door open behind him, a rush of unseasonably cool air washing over his back.

"Am I late?"

Dusty's voice was out of breath, his laugh shaky.

When John glanced over his shoulder at him, Dusty froze, and cringed.

John looked him up and down. The kid was wearing his old army coat. It was brisk outside, but not that cold.

"Who are you?" Tommie Nell sent a frown from John to Dusty.

Rubbing the side of his neck and sending a nervous glance past John to Kelly, Dusty mumbled, "Shorty sent me."

"Shorty?" John asked the same time Tommie Nell did.

"Yeah, you know...Shorty," Dusty confirmed to

Tommie Nell, then slid John a sheepish look. "What are you doing here?"

John passed a hand over his face, covered his mouth and blew frustrated air into his palm. When he dropped it, he said, "What are you doing, kid?"

Dusty shrugged and flashed open his coat. He wore nothing but a pair of white boxers decorated with red hearts. And his tool belt. His chest was flat and smooth. The kid hadn't even filled out yet. "Making an extra fifty bucks."

Tommie Nell grinned.

Kelly groaned.

John's blood pressure hit the roof. "Get in your truck," he told Dusty. He turned to Tommie Nell and Kelly. "Next time try the Yellow Pages."

"Come on, Cap, don't be such a—" Dusty cut himself short when John tapped his left arm.

"Wait a minute," Kelly said, moving toward them and shaking her head as if she'd just awoken from a deep sleep. "You don't think I had anything to do with this."

"What's the holdup?" Mabel and her bulldog frown was one step ahead of Hazel, who was one step ahead of Melva.

"Quit hogging the entertainment, Tommie Nell," Hazel started to say, then stopped dead in her tracks, her eyes widening. "My Lord, there are two of them."

John muttered a curse, then tried to bite it back. Too late. Half the town heard it, judging from the openmouthed astonishment of the two women old enough to be his mother.

"So help me God, Dusty, if you don't get in your

truck this very minute I've a mind to bloody well leave you here with them," John said through gritted teeth. "It ain't gonna be pretty. Trust me."

"Do I still get my fifty bucks?" Dusty asked, eyeing the enthusiastic crowd with increasing misgiving.

John reached into his pocket and pulled out a wad of bills. He didn't know how much was there. More than fifty, he figured. "Here."

"Hey, I don't want your money."

John tried shoving it at him while he walked past Dusty to the door. His friend refused to take it, but after flicking another glance at his audience, he hurried outside after John.

"Hey, Cap, you don't understand. My sister's coming to visit and I needed the extra cash."

John offered him the money one more time, but when Dusty adamantly shook his head, John pocketed the bills, then swung into his Jeep. The kid wasn't his charge. He was over twenty-one. Barely. Dusty didn't owe him any explanations. John inhaled and slowly slid the key into the ignition. "You need overtime, I'll give you all you can handle."

"Yeah, but fifty bucks for only—"

"Dusty?"

"Yeah?"

"Don't be a jackass."

"Yes, sir." Dusty stared at his steel-toed boots. Between the hem of the army green coat and the top of his boots, two inches of skinny white hairy legs were exposed.

Shaking his head, John laughed. "See you tomorrow, kid."

Dusty nodded and got into his battered tan pickup.

Within seconds he'd reversed onto Main Street and peeled out of town.

John noticed one of the kid's taillights was out. He'd have to stop at Ellie Applegate's repair shop and pick up a new one for him. He turned the key and checked behind him for traffic.

"He has a lot of respect for you."

For a moment he thought he'd imagined Kelly's voice. He eased off the accelerator and scanned the sidewalk. Standing in the shadow of Henderson's Bakery's green awning, she watched him.

"Imagine that. Someone doesn't think I'm a shiftless deadbeat." He leaned back in his seat, but left the engine running.

She was silent for nearly a minute before she stepped out of the shadows and under a streetlight. "I owe you an apology."

"Forget it."

"I was wrong." She looked down, her lashes casting long spidery shadows on her pale face. Her hands were slightly unsteady as her fingers picked at the pink-tipped nails. "I don't blame you for being angry." Slowly lifting her gaze, she moved a shoulder. "I was just so…stunned."

"You? I thought you were going to have to scrape me off the floor. The hell with the fuzzy navels, those women need tranquilizers. Industrial strength. The kind they give gorillas."

A small smile curved her mouth. "I've never seen them act like that before."

He shuddered. "Looks like I'd better start going over to the diner in Clarksville."

Her grin broadened. "I suspect by tomorrow they'll all be a whole lot more embarrassed than you were."

"Were? I'm still shaking in my boots."

She laughed. "I don't know. It kind of seemed like you were enjoying the attention."

He gave her a deadly look that not even the dim lighting could disguise.

She laughed harder, while stepping closer to the Jeep. "I think Hazel's glasses are still fogged. I don't know how she's going to get her blueberry pancake batter made for tomorrow morning's rush."

He stared for a moment, then turned off the Jeep engine and laughed. "What's going on in there, anyway?" he asked, nudging his chin in the direction of the town hall.

"It's a shower. For me." Her voice had dipped. More like it was a funeral.

"Ah." He nodded. "And what's a shower without a stripper?"

"I didn't know anything about that. Neither did Ellie or Lana." She crossed her arms over her chest. "That was Tommie Nell's doing. I wish Jimmy Bartlett would break down and marry that woman."

"Right. Marriage solves everything."

"Not everything."

He smiled. "But a nice pretty house will."

"Why are you picking on me? I only came out to say I was sorry."

Good question. Why was he picking on her? Her marriage was none of his business. Hell, *she* was none of his business. He started the engine again. "Go have a good time."

"Wait." Her fingers curled over the ledge of the open Jeep window. "Why did you come?"

"A job estimate."

"For city hall?"

He glanced at the numbers above the door. "This is the right address."

"Who called you?"

He frowned. It was an unusual name. He had it written down. Patting his breast pocket, he said, "A Ms. Honeycare, or something like that."

"Hunyacre? Ona Mae?"

He withdrew his fingers from his pocket. "That's it."

Pursing her lips, she mumbled, "What is she up to?"

"So I take it I won't be getting a job out of this?"

An impish smile lifted the corners of her mouth. "Oh, I imagine you could get enough work to last you into the next decade."

He glanced at the star-studded sky and heaved an exasperated sigh. "Okay, on that note, I'll be moving on."

Laughing, she stepped back from the Jeep. But her fingers lingered on the door and without thinking, he covered her hand with his palm.

A small gasp of surprise escaped her, but she didn't pull back. She stood perfectly still, not even her eyelids moving.

He wrapped his hand around hers until his fingers curled into her palm. Slowly he lifted her hand off the cold metal and brought it to his lips. He pressed a light, feather-soft kiss onto her warm skin.

"Congratulations." He set her palm back atop the

window frame. "I assume that's what you say at a shower."

She looked stiff. Her hand lay at a limp twist where he'd placed it. The rest of her body remained rigid with indecision.

He'd overstepped his bounds. He hadn't meant to. It wasn't as if he'd kissed her on the lips, or even the cheek. This should have been a safe touch. But it wasn't.

Or his entire body wouldn't be reacting. And the feel of her silky skin wouldn't still be taunting his mouth. Knowing there was so much chemistry between them, he knew better than to push the boundary.

Even when John hadn't had a penny to his name, or even a spare shirt to cover his back, he'd always prided himself in being honorable. Having entered this country as an illegal alien had rankled him, even though he'd purposely worked twice as hard as anyone else and had long ago made restitution to Uncle Sam. But how far had he really come when every time he thought of Kelly, there wasn't a damn honorable bone in his body?

Uneasy, he glanced around, hoping there was no witness to that foolish display. Besides, he didn't want to look at her. He didn't want to see her confusion turn to accusation. Bad enough he knew he deserved more than her anger.

Too much silence stretched and he revved the engine. Her fingers immediately slipped away from the Jeep, and he knew he had to quit being a wuss and look at her.

Her expression was blank. She'd make a clever

poker player. But he knew she was going to tell him
to go to hell. Good. He needed to hear that. She
needed to say it.

She used the hand she pulled back to run up her
opposite arm. "What time do you start work tomorrow?"

He exhaled, wary. "Um…around eight."

She nodded, then casually tapped the side of his
door as she stepped away. "I'll see you at the house."

Chapter Eleven

"He's adorable, isn't he?" Lana asked Ellie, who nodded absently and continued stacking gifts on Kelly's kitchen table. Lana immediately turned to Kelly. "Don't you think he's really good-looking?"

Kelly shrugged indifferently. "Maybe. If he'd get a haircut."

"Oh, please, haircut or not. He's...something."

Kelly rolled her eyes heavenward. She did not want to talk about John. That's why she had exited the shower so fast that she'd forgotten most of her gifts. That's why her dear friends had shown up bright and early to bring them over. And to talk about John. Sheesh.

She mentally shook her head. Staying awake, thinking about him half the night had not helped her concentration. That was one of the reasons why she'd made up her mind she would absolutely not see him today. No way, no how. It had been a dumb, impulsive idea. One she'd suggested so he wouldn't know how much that one simple gesture had affected her.

She absentmindedly rubbed the spot on her hand where his lips had touched, and meaningfully eyed

Lana's very pregnant belly. "I thought you were a happily married woman."

Lana's waved her off. "You know I am. I'm just trying to figure out who we can fix him up with."

"You sound like your mother."

"Really?" Lana made a face and left the kitchen to get more things out of the car.

Chuckling, Ellie looked up and watched Lana from the window. "You sure know how to shut her up," she said, then gave Kelly a mischievous sidelong glance. "You do realize that you and John make a really cute couple."

"Get over it, Ellie. I'm marrying Gary." Kelly picked up one of the chocolate doughnuts Lana had brought, stared at it a moment, then dropped it back into the box.

Ellie faked a shiver at Kelly's display of willpower. "You're scaring me."

Kelly couldn't help but smile. She shrugged and poured herself another cup of black coffee. "I'm going to fit into that wedding dress if it kills me."

"Uh-huh."

Kelly sighed, ignoring her, then out of the corner of her eye, saw someone talking to Lana outside. She moved around to the back door and opened it in time to see Ona Mae sprint up the last step.

"I want to talk to you," Kelly told her as the woman marched past her, and spotting the white bakery box, headed straight for it.

"Good. Did you get anything out of him?" Ona Mae asked, stopping to poke at the doughnuts with Lana's discarded hot cocoa spoon. She made a disgusted face. "You girls don't need to be eating this junk."

Kelly closed the box. "Get anything out of whom?"

"That government spy. The one who's here to monitor the aliens."

Her lips pressed together, Ellie glanced at Kelly. "I promised Jasper I'd get to his muffler this morning. It's almost nine now. I'd better head on over to the shop."

"Coward," Kelly mouthed.

Behind the older woman, Ellie grinned and nodded. "See you later, Auntie Om."

Lana ducked her head in the door just as Ellie was about to leave. "Ellie, don't forget you're giving me a ride back to town."

They were both cowards. But that was okay. Kelly wanted to talk with Ona Mae alone, anyway. She waved to her friends. "Thanks for bringing the gifts."

"Tell them to take these doughnuts with them," Ona Mae grumbled as she claimed a seat.

"Don't worry. I'm not going to eat them." For emphasis, Kelly swept the box aside, then sat across the table from the older woman.

"You still fixin' to fit into Sunshine's dress?"

Kelly nodded. That dress was the only traditional thing her mother owned. Kelly was determined to wear it. "Ona Mae, why did you trick John Cappel into coming to the shower last night?"

The woman reared her head back slightly, her eyebrows dipping in a befuddled frown…as though Kelly was the one who was a little daft. "I needed lots of witnesses. You didn't think I was going to go talk to him alone, did you?''

"Talk to him about what?"

"I want to know what he intends on doing about the alien population. He works for the government. We pay his salary. We have a right to know." Ona Mae's disgruntled gaze fell on the bakery box. "Did I see a chocolate one in there?"

"It isn't frozen. It doesn't count."

"Don't be smart with me, young lady."

Kelly couldn't hold back her laughter any longer. "I'm just trying to help."

"You're awfully smug for someone who can't find Purple Bunny," Ona Mae said, sitting back with a devilish gleam in her eye that told Kelly her friend was up to no good.

Kelly abruptly stopped laughing. "Okay, Aunt Om, 'fess up. You know where Purple Bunny is, don't you?"

"Oh, it's Aunt Om, now, is it?"

"You're the one who told me to call you Ona Mae," Kelly snapped. "Now, do you know something about Purple Bunny?"

"Maybe."

Kelly's thoughts spun and scattered like sugar in a cotton candy machine. This was totally unlike Ona Mae. Although she could be difficult with some people, she was always agreeable with Kelly. "This is important, Ona Mae," she said quietly.

"So is finding out about this government guy." Ona Mae patted her hand. "You scratch my back, I'll scratch yours."

"Aunt Om!"

"Now, don't give me those puppy dog eyes and go getting your feelings hurt."

Too late. Kelly's feelings were beyond hurt. They were numb. This wasn't at all like Ona Mae.

"I didn't say I know where that ugly critter is," Ona Mae continued. "I said I'd help you find him."

She was hedging. She knew something. Kelly was sure of it. Only she didn't know why Aunt Om was suddenly being so stubborn with her. "All right. I'll talk to John."

"When?"

Oh, God. She didn't want to talk to John.

Liar. There was that small irritating voice again, the one that had taunted her last night every time she tried to pull the covers over her head.

Kelly let out a breath. "I'll talk to him today."

"Think he'll tell you anything?"

"He'll talk." She'd make up a whopper of a story, she decided. Something that Ona Mae would feel was worth trading Purple Bunny for.

Ona Mae pursed her lips in a contemplative fashion. "How come you're so cozy with him?"

Kelly's laugh was short, indignant, humorless. She stood. "I'm not cozy with him. He's working on my house." She reached for the coffee carafe. Her hand shook slightly and when her gaze flickered to Ona Mae, she saw that the older woman was staring at her with intense interest.

Kelly abandoned the carafe and dried her clammy hands on the kitchen towel. "Everybody knows how slow some contractors can be. I have to stay on top of him."

Ona Mae giggled and Kelly shot her a startled look.

Surely she wasn't reacting to the way Kelly had phrased that. But from the sly gleam in Auntie Om's eyes, that's exactly what she was reacting to. Kelly's cheeks heated.

"With Gary being out of town so much, somebody has had to keep tabs on..." She'd almost said John. Best to leave this impersonal. "The construction."

Ona Mae nodded, not a hint of conviction on her amused face.

Kelly started to defend herself further and quickly closed her mouth, realizing she'd only add fuel to the fire.

Ona Mae stared at a speck of doughnut glaze sitting on the bakery box. Absently she blotted it with her forefinger and brought it to the tip of her tongue. "Why is Gary out of town so much lately? I'd think that boy would have too much to do with the wedding being so close."

Her expression said more than her words. Annoyingly, it echoed Kelly's thoughts. "He's not getting cold feet, if that's what you think."

"Of course he is."

"As endearing as I find your bluntness, you're wrong." Kelly's sarcasm was tempered by the immediate recollection of the night she'd seen Gary's car at John's cabin. She bit her lip. She'd been burning to tell someone, to have them reassure her that Gary's small lie had meant nothing. But was she prepared for the alternative? Swallowing her fear, she added, "I mean, he's probably just getting the usual jitters like everyone does."

"Like you?"

"I wouldn't call it jitters." Kelly stared down at

her manicure. If you could call it that. She'd made such a mess of the polish, chipping at it throughout the night, that she'd finally had to remove all the enamel. This was the first time her nails had been colorless in years.

Ona Mae allowed a nerve-racking amount of time to pass and when Kelly finally forced herself to look up, the other woman drew her eyebrows together in a thoughtful expression and said, "I may have underestimated those aliens."

Kelly half laughed, half sobbed, grateful the subject had changed to Ona Mae's favorite and much safer topic of conversation. "Why?"

"Fate," she said, eyeing Kelly in such an odd way that it gave her the willies. "Go see your John Cappel, child. He may have some answers."

OKAY. KELLY SUCKED in a huge gulp of fresh mountain air, prepared to practice another round of deep breathing exercises. She knew her nerves were shot from lack of sleep, her way-too-vivid imagination and from Ona Mae's unsettling remarks. This didn't mean she had to overreact.

None of this knowledge helped.

She stared at her nearly finished house...and the bare area of gravel where John's Jeep should be. And she wanted to scream.

She glanced at the digital clock on her dashboard. Nine-thirty. Angling her wrist, she saw the hand on her watch move to thirty-two past the hour. Where the hell was he? He said he'd be here at eight.

Even though it was a relatively cool day, the back of her neck had grown clammy and her palms were too slick to rest on the steering wheel. She hated when these minor panic attacks started. Often there was no reason for them. What bothered her even more was the flaring of her temper in reaction. Like right now.

But she wasn't going to let her ill temperament get the better of her this time. She'd outgrown the childish foolishness that had earned her such a horrid reputation in high school. Drumming her fingers, she started counting backward from one hundred.

By the time she got to seventy-eight, she saw his Jeep in her rearview mirror.

Vaguely she recalled that sixty-two did not come before seventy-eight but that was her last tango with sanity. Breathing ceased, period. And the pressure in her chest expanded with frightening speed.

She dragged a damp palm down her khaki shorts and jumped out of her car before he'd barely gotten his door open.

"Good morning," he said, smiling.

"Where the hell were you?"

He snorted, his grin fading. "I guess it's not such a good one."

"You said you'd be here at eight."

"Yeah." He shot her a funny look before closing the door and heading toward the back of the Jeep.

"Don't walk away from me like that."

"Kelly." He stopped, his expression a combination of irritation and confusion. "What's wrong?"

"Is it too much to expect you to be punctual?" Her voice had raised an octave and she knew she sounded shrewish. She struggled for a deep breath, and settled for a shallow one. Under John's concerned gaze, she took another.

Feeling slightly more in control, she glanced around, thankful that the other men weren't here to witness this. Most of their work was done and she was grateful they hadn't gotten a glimpse of the old Kelly.

Then her eyes met John's and her breath stuttered. Too bad he had. "You said you'd be here at eight," she said more quietly.

He watched her for a moment, then slowly moved toward her. "I was here at eight. I had to run to town for some supplies. Dusty is at the airport picking up his sister." He stopped a foot away from her. "This isn't about what time I start work, is it, Kelly?" He took her hand and softly stroked the inside of her wrist. "Tell me what's wrong."

There was nothing sexual about the gesture. It was meant as nothing more than comfort. Kelly swallowed hard.

Oh, God. She didn't want to start crying in front of him, too. She tried to pull away.

He wouldn't let her.

A sob clogged her throat, threatening her last shred of composure, and she yanked one more time.

He still wouldn't let go.

"I don't know," she said, her anger starting to return.

"Think about it for a minute," he said softly. "I'm not going anywhere."

"Yeah, well, I wish you would." She experimentally wiggled her shackled wrist.

A faint grin tugged at his mouth. "That's not what you said a minute ago."

She half laughed. It sounded suspiciously like a

sob. But she wasn't going to cry anymore, she thought, and gazed into his kind blue eyes. Then again, maybe she would.

"Sunshine," she whispered, and forced back the lump in her throat. He was peering at her, squinting a little as if he were trying to understand, and then one dark brow lifted and comprehension warmed his eyes.

She wished she understood as well as he suddenly seemed to. She hadn't even been thinking about her mother. Heaven only knew what brought on that answer.

Kelly sniffed. That was a lie. She knew. Too many nights she'd waited for her mother to come home, deathly afraid she never would. Sunshine had never meant to hurt her. When she'd tell Kelly she would be back soon, she must have figured two hours or two days meant no difference to an eight-year-old. She was wrong.

His hand loosened around her wrist, and when she would have stepped away he put his arm around her and gave her a hug. Just a brief one, around the shoulders, but it felt so comforting, so right, she leaned into him.

After a fleeting hesitation his other arm came up around her and he brought her solidly against his chest.

"Do you want to talk about it?" he asked, his voice soft and low, stirring the tendrils of hair near her ear.

"Do you charge by the hour?" she asked, with a small unsure laugh.

"Yup. Or three hugs for a half hour."

As nice as it was being snuggled against his chest, her right palm molding the firm curve of muscled skin over his heart, his hand stroking her hair, she moved back. Not because she wanted to, but because she had to put some distance between them.

She suddenly felt too vulnerable and needy. His concern touched that small place in her heart where she'd buried hurt feelings for so long. She couldn't trust what kind of reaction his probing questions and eyes would provoke.

All her life, friends and acquaintances teased her about her temper. Sometimes they criticized her, sometimes they scolded, and more often they simply discussed her flaws behind her back. But no one had asked her what was wrong before.

Clearly sensing her discomfort, he also eased back. But he ducked his head, forcing eye contact. That wasn't much better. She saw the concern again, growing in intensity, and her insides got mushier than grits swimming in warm butter.

Kelly shrugged one shoulder. "There's really not much to say. You've probably heard enough to know about where I grew up." She shrugged again. "Respect for punctuality is somewhat lacking in a commune."

"I thought you grew up here in Bachelor Falls."

"I did. Sunshine inherited a farm from my grandparents. She turned it into a commune."

He leaned against the Jeep as if he were settling in for a long story. As much as she appreciated his nonthreatening posture, she was going to disappoint him.

"That's it," she said.

"Where is it? What happened to the commune?"

"I still live there. Although it has—" she laughed "—changed."

His eyebrows shot up. "Your little house?"

"It wasn't so little until a few years ago. There were a bunch of shabby add-ons I had torn down. As word spread that Sunshine's home was open to one and all, a lot of drifters started taking up residence. And everyone pitched in and kept building and adding."

"I'd think that would've been fun for a child. Sounds like a lot of freedom."

"Too much." Looking away, she closed her eyes and lifted her face toward the sun. Its rays were warm and soothing on her skin. The air smelled so clean and fresh, and she felt her nerves start to calm down.

"However you were raised, look how well you turned out."

She brought her eyes back to him to see if he was being sarcastic or facetious, but found nothing but sincerity in his expression. "You mean, neurotic?"

He smiled. "I'd call it a little high-strung."

"Yeah. Right." Her lips curved for a brief moment. "I didn't have a bad childhood. I'm not blaming my mother. She was fun. Even though a lot of the kids teased me, they were jealous that she was so liberal."

"She just didn't believe in a white picket fence."

"Oh, no, she believed in it all right. She just thought it should surround the entire county."

"Which left little time for her daughter."

Kelly stared down at her toes. At least her nervous picking had spared her pink toenails. She curled them over the top of her tan sandals into the gravel until the tiny rocks dug into her skin. "She used to go away sometimes. I never knew if it would be for a few hours or a few days."

She saw his hand reach out to grasp her forearm before she actually felt him make contact, and her breath caught. He stroked his palm up to her elbow, then cupping it, pulled her gently toward him.

"That's why being on time is so important to you," he said, his voice softening, his gaze intensifying. "Or old feelings of panic are stirred. That's perfectly understandable."

"What were you, some kind of shrink in a former life?" she murmured, her eyes beginning to widen as his face grew alarmingly close. Speaking of panic...

She took an ungraceful step forward, slid in the gravel and lost her footing.

His arms were quick to circle her as he said, "No, a bartender." His low chuckle vibrated from his chest, stroking her cheek as she came to rest against his steady heartbeat.

She shouldn't be here in this position. Letting this man hold her. But it had been a long time since she'd been held. Really held. Not just the quick pats and pecks she got from Gary.

Gary.

He didn't deserve this.

She straightened. Or at least she tried to. John wasn't in any hurry to cooperate. He hugged her tighter.

Putting up a hand, she pressed a palm to his chest and gently levered herself away. "John, please."

He promptly dropped his arms but made no move to step back. "Are you okay?"

"Well, yeah. I just..." She stared warily at him as his hand lifted again, this time toward her face. "What are you doing?"

The pad of his thumb brushed her cheek and she felt moisture. She blinked as panic swelled in her throat. Had she been crying without realizing it? She dashed a hand across her face. It was dry.

"I got it," he said quietly.

Okay, maybe it wasn't as bad as she'd feared. One lone tear was explainable. "Allergies," she mumbled.

A slow, knowing grin curved his lips, making her face start to heat up. "To me?"

"I think so."

He nodded. "I wasn't trying to be pushy. You looked like you needed a hug."

"I've been having a rough morning." It wasn't a lie. She didn't do well with so little sleep. "Which brings me to the reason I'm here. Aunt Om."

Confusion creased his face. She paused a moment and noticed that his attention had drawn to her hands. They still trembled slightly. Her gaze immediately returned to his face as she entwined her traitorous fingers.

Pity. Now that she was calming down, she recognized the despised emotion etched in the lines bracketing his mouth, the shadow darkening his eyes.

Anger wove a purposeful path down her spine and it was easy to move farther back, to shake the useless neediness that had made her so stupidly vulnerable.

"Aunt Om?" he asked when she'd let too much time pass.

"Ona Mae Hunyacre." The name came out much sharper than she'd intended. She lifted her chin. "The woman who'd asked you to go to city hall last night," she added unnecessarily because he was already nodding.

There was a sudden change in mood. John was obviously no longer confused. He looked mad.

Chapter Twelve

"You want to tell me what just happened here," he said, feeling his jaw start to clench.

John wasn't half as angry with her as he was with himself. No, he had no business wanting to kiss her. He had no business touching her, period. But it wasn't as if he'd been planning her seduction.

He stretched his neck from one side to the other. He hadn't consciously planned it, anyway. Something was troubling her. She'd even looked a little unsteady on her feet at one point. And he'd wanted to help. That was all.

Now she was staring at him as though he was some kind of pervert. Well, she hadn't exactly run from him, either.

Bloody hell. He didn't know what it was about her that brought out this white-knight crap in him. Her of all women. She didn't need his help or sympathy. He doubted Kelly needed anyone's.

"Nothing happened," she said, her voice rising several defensive notches. "I'm trying to tell you about Ona Mae."

"It's not like I kissed you."

"What?"

"Okay. It was obvious that I wanted to. I'll concede that. But I didn't." He turned away and headed around the rear of the Jeep to retrieve the supplies he'd picked up. "I drew the line."

"You *wanted* to kiss me?"

He froze, his hand on the latch. She still stood near the driver's door and he couldn't see her face. But there was no mistaking her wistful tone. Or maybe the damn squeaky latch hinge had distorted her voice.

He ducked his head to the side. Her eyes were wide, questioning. She looked slightly confused...a little pleased. He frowned. "Run that by me again."

Her chin lifted again. "Or were you just feeling sorry for me?"

He laughed. "Lady, if I feel sorry for anyone, it's me," he said as he reached into the Jeep and hauled out a two-by-four.

"How's that?"

"I'd show you except you're engaged and I can't take any more torture."

She squinted suspiciously at him. Her gaze started to lower, then swung back to his face in furious haste. She blinked several times, her mouth starting to open.

It wasn't hard to keep his misguided amusement at bay. He was as frustrated and disgusted with himself as he was entertained by the obvious and comical conflict of emotions parading across her disbelieving face. He dropped the two-by-four on the ground and hauled out a burlap sack full of nails.

"You're talking about that chemistry issue again, aren't you?" she said matter-of-factly as she walked around the Jeep.

He stooped to hoist up some of the things he'd set on the ground and watched her pink-tipped big toe draw patterns in the gravel. The action didn't seem nervous—on the contrary, it seemed almost sensual, and he wondered what other interesting things she could do with her toes.

Bloody hell. "You need to move."

"Well, excuse me." Her pink toes shuffled back a few inches. Then she crouched down to pick up the sack of nails. Her khaki shorts rode up her thigh, the cuff ending several inches higher than normal to expose a strip of skin he'd bet rarely saw the light of day. Across the band of paler flesh, a smattering of tiny golden hairs glistened under the morning sun.

Then she stood with the sack in her arms, and the temptation was gone. But not his desire to see more. To see all of her.

"Don't you have some bookkeeping to do, or something?" he asked, his irritation plain.

Maybe she was right. Maybe he did feel sorry for her. Maybe that was what all this odd jumble of feeling he had for her was about. After all, he didn't really know her.

"Do you realize we never finish any conversation we start?" she asked, and fell into step beside him as he headed toward the front door of the house. "First, we were supposed to discuss the completion date of the house, then we were going to talk about chemistry—"

He groaned and walked faster.

She did a little hop to keep up. "Is something wrong?" she asked, and when he didn't answer, out of the corner of his eye, he saw her shrug. "And now, I still have to explain about Ona Mae."

"Keep yakking and I won't get this house done at all."

"You don't have to get huffy. I wasn't criticizing. I was merely making an observation."

"I'm not huffy. I'm busy."

"Oh. Shall I come back at lunch?"

"No."

"After you knock off?"

"No."

She heaved a loud annoyed sigh. "Then when?"

"I'd invite you to my place, but you'd probably stand me up again. How's that for a subject we never finished?"

He regretted his words as soon as they left his mouth, and he felt even worse watching the color drain from her face. Although her earlier discourtesy as a no-show had bothered him, he hadn't planned on bringing up the matter. But now, understanding how much punctuality meant to her, the old wound must have unwittingly been opened.

"What happened that night, Kelly? You didn't show up, didn't call." He lightened his tone. "What's up with that?"

"I tried to call. I...something came up. Some plans I'd made with Lana and Ellie and I—" The color had returned to her face with a vengeance, staining her cheeks a bright pink. "You aren't listed with directory assistance."

"You could have said something the next day."

"I should have. You're right. I don't remember why I didn't," she said, looking away.

Her fluttering gaze wasn't the only tip-off that she was lying. Or at least wasn't being totally honest. Something else was definitely bothering her. He sure hoped it wasn't…

Frowning, he caught her arm and forced her to face him. "You didn't think I was going to put the moves on you, did you?"

"Of course not," she said, and although she shook away from his hold, he didn't take that as a sign of a lie.

He believed her. There was something in the exasperated tone of her voice that convinced him. But then, why? He studied her openly for several minutes. But her narrow, guarded eyes told him nothing. Nor did the defensive hunch of her shoulders. Probably better to let the matter drop.

"Okay, okay," she said, scowling. "I was afraid of me, okay? Happy? I was afraid *I'd* jump your bones."

Miffed, Kelly folded her arms across her chest and frowned harder. Not even the hilarious look of terrified shock that crossed his face loosened her up. Part of her still couldn't believe she'd just said that, except making that ludicrous claim was better than him knowing she knew the truth. That Gary had gone to John's cabin to express misgivings about his marriage to her. Gary wouldn't dare share his feelings with anyone else in town and risk his words hitting the party line. Ross may have been a possibility once, but he was Ellie's husband now. No, if Gary had felt the need to spill his guts, John would have been the logical choice. Gary seemed to genuinely like the guy.

Maybe he'd even asked John to slow down work on the house.

This was a new thought and she bit down on her lip. Rejection hurt, no matter which way you sliced it. She refocused on John's still-stunned face and decided she wasn't one bit sorry for coming up with that absurd claim of wanting to jump his bones.

His jaw tensed, one dark eyebrow dipped and he raised a hand to massage his left temple. The sight of his long lean fingers slowly making stroking movements made her recall his hands on her and her insides fluttered.

Okay, so maybe it wasn't a totally absurd claim. But she was sure the notion had only occurred to her out of hurt. She'd gone over the possible reasons Gary had lied to her dozens of times in her mind. And in the end, she kept coming up with the same answer. Gary's feet were getting so frigid, it was going to take increased global warming to thaw them out.

John's surprise faded and he started to look a little smug. "I see you finally understand the chemistry concept."

She wanted to hit him. Not hard. Just enough to stun him again. And, admittedly, to let out her frustration. But that was the old, childish Kelly's thinking. Allowing fear to get the better of her, prompting her to strike out at anything in her path.

She'd stopped that behavior a long time ago. She had no desire to resurrect it. But...maybe she should make him squirm...let him know she knew Gary had been to his cabin while claiming to be out of town. But John wouldn't squirm. He'd just look at her with pity again. And Kelly couldn't bear that.

"I understood the chemistry concept all along. I was just playing with you," she said with a casual shrug. "A couple of years ago I had a thing for Shorty. Last year it was Ralph. I'll get over this...this nonsense, too."

The stunned look was back again, first widening then narrowing his eyes. She couldn't imagine how he felt to be thrown in the same category with Shorty and Ralph, she thought, giving his muscled chest and tight worn jeans a quick once-over. They were both nice enough guys, but...

Why did she do this to herself?

Swallowing, she abruptly raised her gaze to his face and smiled brightly. "Okay. Now that we have that out of the way, let me tell you about Ona Mae."

John dropped the supplies and nudged them to the side with his boot while trying to shake the cloying fog from his brain. Actually, he didn't think they'd gotten one blasted thing out of the way. But from the way she was acting, he figured she didn't have a single intention of discussing what was really eating at her.

"Okay, I'm listening," he said, and tried to do just that even though his mind was racing.

"She thinks you're here because of the Bostians," Kelly said, shaking her head. "I mean, she thinks the government sent you, but for the purpose of monitoring the Bostians."

He stared intently at her. She looked okay. Her cheeks were no longer flushed, and a wide range of emotions weren't playing leapfrog across her face anymore. But she still wasn't making any sense. "Bostians?"

"The aliens? From Bost?"

No question. She was totally stressed out. She stood there, looking at him as if she were amazed he could be so clueless. Hadn't her friends noticed how frayed her nerves were getting?

"She does, huh?" Absently he scratched his chest and watched her gaze draw to the action. He didn't know what to say next. If he suggested she see a doctor, she'd probably jump down his throat.

Kelly nodded, her gaze appearing to be helplessly transfixed by the motion of his hand. So he kept scratching. "And now I think she may be holding Purple Bunny hostage," she said.

"Bloody hell. This is bad."

He hadn't realized he'd spoken out loud until she dragged her attention up and looked at him with an odd hint of satisfaction in her eyes. "I know. And I bet you thought I was overreacting."

"Of course not."

"Well, good, because now you're involved, too. She wants me to find out what your mission is. I either tell her what she wants to hear or prove she's wrong, or I may never see Purple Bunny again."

"Okay." He glanced around and patted his back pocket at the same time. He needed a piece of paper to leave Dusty a note.

"Are you paying attention? Will you help me with this?"

"Yes." His gaze again riveted to her face. She seemed calm. Her earlier nervousness was gone. Even her hands weren't shaky anymore. "How do you want to handle this?"

"Well, I think we need to iron out some facts."

Her hand trembled again, and he heard the hesitation in her voice. And then with more resolve, she said, "She's even starting to hallucinate."

"How so?"

Hesitation again. "She thought she saw Gary here last week when everyone knew he was out of town."

Her words came out in a rush, as if she were afraid of not getting them all out at once. And then she just stood there, looking wary, oddly defensive, and yet scared. Her stance had changed subtly, too; clearly, she was waiting for him to say something.

Hell, what was he supposed to say? *Look, Kelly, I think you either need to sleep for a week or visit a good shrink.*

"Did you see Gary last week?" she asked slowly.

He frowned, looked to the left and watched a tiny gray sparrow perch on the kitchen windowsill. "No," he said, truthfully. "Wait a minute. I did." He looked back at her. She seemed a little pale. He was going to have to take her home, or maybe her friends could help him get her to a doctor. "At your house. Remember? He came home the night I was there. But that's the only time."

That obviously wasn't the answer she wanted or expected. Anger was the first emotion to cross her face, and then the parade started again, showcasing everything from disappointment to sadness.

"Are you sure?" she asked, her voice sounding anything but normal. "Auntie Om thought she saw him at your cabin."

"Positive." Whoever the hell Auntie Om was, she sure as heck hadn't been to his cabin, either. Shoving a hand into his right front pocket, he withdrew a matchbook. Damn. He wasn't going to get much writing on this.

"What are you looking for?" Suspicion glittered in her eyes as she cocked her head to the side and studied him.

"I need to leave Dusty a note."

"You're leaving?"

"We have to go talk to Anna Mae, don't we?"

"Oh. It's Ona Mae, but I don't think you actually have to talk to her yourself," she said, backing away from him.

"Wait. Don't you want me to explain to her what I'm doing with the aliens? And that I didn't see Gary last week," he said in a soothing tone.

He didn't want to make any sudden moves and spook her. No way was he letting her get in a car and drive down the hill by herself. Her strange behavior was probably nothing worse than a case of jangled nerves, but he hadn't seen anything like this outside of combat, and he knew how much damage stress could do to a person.

"No, you don't need to speak to her yourself. I—I'll just tell her your government mail has to do with a sweepstakes or something. You back me up if she doesn't believe me."

My government mail? He forced a smile. "Of course I'll back you up. We'll do it right now and get it over with. And Ona Mae can give you back Purple Bunny."

"No. You have to stay here and work on my house."

"Everything will still be here when I get back,

Kelly. Don't worry about a thing." He put an arm around her shoulders and she jumped.

"You're acting very strangely," she said, issuing him a challenging glance as she sidestepped him. "You wouldn't be hiding anything, would you?"

He almost laughed. Maybe he should admit he was harboring aliens in his cabin. Maybe then Kelly would be shocked into seeing reason. "No," he said. "I'm not hiding anything. Come on, honey, let's go talk to this Ona Mae."

He put out his hand and her openmouthed stare dropped from his face to his palm. Then her dull topaz eyes slowly traveled back up to his face. The endearment probably caught her off guard. He hadn't used it for that purpose. The word had sort of fallen out of his mouth. He was worried about her. This wasn't the Kelly he was used to dealing with.

"Kelly?" he said to reclaim her attention. Her gaze had wandered off somewhere out the window. She didn't respond right away, but when her eyes finally met his, he said, "You're tired. You've been under a lot of strain lately."

She nodded, and with mixed feelings, he realized the fight had drained from her. But as much as he hated seeing this defeated look, he was glad she'd calmed down.

"You've been worried about the house getting finished on time," he said gently, keeping his hand extended. "And I know about all the free bookkeeping you do."

Annoyance flashed in her eyes. "You should know better than to listen to idle gossip. It's not free."

He tempered the smile tugging at his lips. She

didn't want people to know she was a softy. But everyone over the age of sixty who lived in Bachelor Falls knew Kelly wouldn't charge them a dime for her services. She'd accept a free meal at the diner or a dozen doughnuts from the bakery from time to time. But that was all. He'd heard talk from more than one source.

Stubbornly she folded her arms across her chest and ignored his outstretched hand. As if reading his mind, she said, "Mabel doesn't make much of a profit and she keeps sending money to her deadbeat daughter in St. Louis. And the Hendersons had a fire a few years ago. They got scammed by their insurance agent and they haven't quite recovered."

"I'm not criticizing you," he said, and pulled back his hand to run it through his hair. "It's admirable to help out your neighbors. One of the good things you learned from communal living, I'm sure," he said, and she glared at him. "What?"

He'd upset her again. Bartering for services wasn't a bad way to live, and she'd probably unconsciously picked up some of her mother's habits. But somehow he didn't think he'd win any points by emphasizing that observation.

He appealed to her by putting out his hand again. "I think you're tired from overextending yourself. Let's take the day off. We'll do something together. Maybe we'll have a picnic. Or even better, drive over to Branson, have lunch there and pick up some more molding at the same time."

Her expression softened and he took advantage of her brief uncertainty by ducking his head to snag her full attention. "We could talk to Ona Mae first and settle up with her. I'll swear to her that I've never seen an alien in my life, and I haven't seen Gary in almost two weeks.''

She winced.

What had he done now? "Kelly? How about it?''

She hesitated for a moment, briefly closed her eyes, then surprised him by laying her palm across his. "Okay,'' she whispered, stepping closer. "But I don't want to talk about Ona Mae. I want you to kiss me.''

Chapter Thirteen

Kelly waited for the guilt to swamp her, half hoping it would make her pull back and force her to run to her car. There was still time to pretend she was kidding, that she wasn't drowning in desperation to feel his lips against hers.

She waited for surprise to cross his face, too, or at the very least condemnation. But he only stared at her with a blank expression, as if unsure he'd heard her correctly.

She still had time to turn away. He wouldn't challenge her, or humiliate her if she backed out. That wasn't John's style.

But she didn't want to back out. She wanted very much to kiss him. And if she felt any guilt at all, it was for harboring a small secret hope that he'd lied about Gary being at his cabin. Because if he did, then she'd know for sure where Gary stood as far as their upcoming marriage was concerned.

She wanted to kiss him all right. Enough to blame Gary's rejection and her own fear to do it. It didn't even matter that deep down she'd known Gary wanted out. She was disgusted with herself for being so weak. But even her disgust and disappointment couldn't dissuade her from wanting this kiss.

"John?" She moved closer, yet prepared herself for his possible rebuke. If he rebuffed her, it would, of course, jab her pride. But she'd also understand.

He squeezed her hand. "Kelly." He said her name softly, an indulgent smile hovering at the corners of his mouth. "You're tired and a little upset and—"

"Yes, I'm both those things. But I still want to kiss you."

"You're making this so hard."

She hoped so. Although she wasn't sure she wanted to go *that* far. A grin blossomed in the wake of her thoughts and she tried to tamp it down.

"What?" he asked, his lips giving into the smile.

"You don't want to know."

He nudged her chin up. "Yeah, I do."

"Trust me on this, okay?" she said, still trying to lose the silly grin. Noticing that his gaze was fixed intently on her mouth, she promptly sobered and moistened her parched lips.

"I trust you," he said. "Do you trust me when I tell you that you really need some rest?"

"Uh-huh," she said, and inched closer, wondering if he knew he was fueling her determination by absently stroking the inside of her wrist.

"I don't want to take advantage of that fact," he muttered, and she knew he was weakening by the hoarseness of his voice.

"Then let me take advantage of you," she whispered.

John stared, his confusion eclipsed only by the strong flare of desire darkening his eyes. He stopped stroking her wrist and the first needle of panic pricked her confidence.

She'd already told herself she wouldn't blame him for rejecting her. He had every right to put a stop to this recklessness, while she had no rights at all.

He dropped her hand. Her heart nose-dived.

"Look, John, I'm—"

She had no chance to let him off the hook. His hand came up to cup her jaw and his mouth covered hers with such a fierce swiftness he literally stole her breath.

She gasped and he swallowed the sound, pushing his tongue between her lips, hooking his arm around her waist to haul her body flush against his.

There was nothing gentle about his movements, which both surprised her and made her instantly so hot and moist she wasn't sure what was happening anymore. She tasted his desperation and her own excitement as she wound her arms around his neck and her breasts pushed against his hard chest.

His hand continued to span her jaw, the tips of his fingers probing her nape as his head slanted, giving his tongue better and deeper access.

She brought up one leg, her knee rubbing outside his thigh, letting her shorts bunch up nearly to her panties. He lowered the hand at her waist to cup her bottom, urging her impossibly closer to him.

Kelly felt his rigid desire press against her belly. Off in the distance she heard an odd grating sound, then realized it was fingernails scraping denim—her nails clawing the seat of his jeans.

In her blind excitement, one hand had slipped from around his neck to caress his backside, pulling him closer, too. Any other time she would have been mortified at her boldness. But she'd never ever been kissed like this before and she didn't want the earthy sensation to end.

But it did.

Almost as quickly as he'd started to kiss her, he stopped.

Then in slow motion, he raised his head, his glazed, troubled eyes cautiously finding hers. His breathing was ragged, matching hers, and he took two silent gulps of air.

She stared up at him, suddenly frightened by the glum regret she saw furrowing his brows. Wanting to say something that would ease the tension already starting to spin its web, she touched her tongue to her nervous, drying lips. He followed the action with his gaze, briefly closed his eyes, and groaned.

When he started to jerk away, she realized that she still had one leg raised up against his thigh. His brusque movement made the denim seam of his jeans chafe her bare skin and she winced.

He blinked down at her leg as she lowered it. A thin red mark branded her skin where she'd pressed herself to him. As soon as her foot touched ground and her shorts fell into place, it was no longer visible.

John didn't hesitate to look up. Their eyes met. He shoved a hand through his hair. "Kelly, I'm sorry."

She swallowed. "Why?"

"I didn't mean to…for things to get out of hand."

"I wasn't exactly crying uncle."

His mouth lifted in a brief lopsided grin. "Maybe you should have."

She shook her head. "I'm not sorry about what just happened. And if you recall, I asked for it."

He snorted. "If *you* recall, you didn't ask for *that*."

She should back off. He was giving her a chance to play the injured party, to keep a shred of her dignity intact. Maybe it would be better for both of them if she did. Maybe it wasn't too late to salvage their professional relationship.

He was still hard.

She blinked and tried not to look. But he was straining against the faded denim fly where the fabric had grown thin and soft with age. And she was getting steamy again just knowing he still wanted her.

"Yes, I did," she blurted.

The heat moved from her belly to her face. She knew she could do nothing about the color filling her cheeks, and she lifted her chin in defiance.

He was trying not to smile. His eyebrows slanted in a stern expression, but the corners of his mouth twitched before he forced his lips into a grim line. "It's not too late to forget anything happened."

"No?" She'd be offended if she thought he was telling the truth. "I'm having a little trouble with that."

He blew out some air. "Okay. Any suggestions?"

"Kiss me again."

"Kelly." He took an automatic step back.

She'd really shocked him this time. Not only shocked him, but she scared the hell out of him, judging by his waning color. This knowledge did nothing for her own confidence. "I mean, only if you want to."

A slow smile curved one side of his mouth. "You're going to be the bloody death of me."

She truly had disconcerted him. His accent always emerged when he was agitated or distracted. She smiled, liking the sound of it, and moved slowly toward him.

He didn't retreat, which she took as a sign she was welcome, but a small case of nerves prompted her to fill the silence. "Are we still going to Branson?"

Her question didn't work. It was met with more silence. Loud, uncomfortable silence. And the instant misgiving she saw spread across his face made her sorry she'd asked what she thought was a casual question.

She stopped and entwined her hands. One look of pity and she'd leave. Without so much as a head turn.

He smiled and reached out a hand. Circling her wrist with his fingers, he pulled her hands apart and urged her toward him. She stumbled on the last step and put her palm against his chest for balance. His heart beat strong and steady under her hand.

"Sure, we'll go to Branson," he said, nudging her chin until her upturned face met his. Lightly he brushed his lips across hers. Just when she thought he'd break contact, he exerted some pressure. But the kiss was still brief and gentle and not very satisfying.

He pulled back and smiled, his eyes trained intently on her face. "I've been meaning to get there." At her puzzled look, he added, "Branson. I wanted to see it before I leave the area."

His reminder couldn't have been more obvious. Kelly tried to smile back as she shifted away and tugged self-consciously at her wrinkled shorts. But the joy and exhilaration had left her.

THE FIRST HOUR into their drive was filled with silence. That suited Kelly fine. She had a lot to think about. And even more guilt to rationalize.

She cast a furtive glance at John's somber profile. He certainly was in no mood to talk. She wondered why he even bothered insisting that they come together. When she'd been tempted to beg out of the trip, he'd pointed out that she had to select some new molding anyway, and that this trip could be considered business.

Not that she had let him know she'd had second thoughts about accompanying him. She'd been careful not to let her hurt show. It wasn't as if she had any right to feel the ache that squeezed her heart.

John was leaving before the end of summer. He wanted to be footloose and fancy-free. And there was no reason for him not to feel that way. Least of all for her sake. She was supposed to marry Gary.

Just thinking about her fiancé stung, and when John tossed her a curious glance, she realized she'd actually flinched. Sticking her hand out the open window, she pretended to adjust the side mirror.

For miles behind them, a forest of trees in varying shades of spring green stretched clear back to Bachelor Falls. The road had been narrow and winding and Kelly knew they were in for at least another hour of curves and dips before they would get to Branson. It had been a long time since she'd made the trip and she'd forgotten how carsick she could get. But so far, she was doing okay. Well, as okay as a guilt hangover would allow.

She was glad about one thing, though. She was finally being forced to face reality. Although deep down she'd known for a while that Gary was afraid of marriage, she'd convinced herself he'd get over it, lied to herself that it was change in general of which he was most afraid. That was a reaction she understood. She'd known forever that she would marry Gary, and deviation from that belief scared the hell out of her.

Now it was time to face her fear. And oddly, it no longer seemed as scary a prospect as it once had. She thought about the nearly finished house, the wedding invitations that had gone out in the mail last week, and swallowed a lump of nausea. Then again, maybe she was still lying to herself.

"We are going the right way, aren't we?" John frowned at the short stretch of road that lay ahead. More trees, more twists and turns, which served to make the route deceptive. They had even farther to go than he thought.

"So that's why you wanted me along. You needed a navigator." *Better learn how to get where you're going, buster, if you plan on seeing the world.* The nasty thought nearly made it to her lips. She coughed.

The mocking glance he gave her made her consider the tone of her voice when she lightly added, "We're going the right way. We should be there within a half hour or so."

"No wonder no one from Bachelor Falls is so hot to run over here for a little entertainment. It may only be eighty-something miles, but these damn roads are too winding to let you make decent time.''

His querulous tone sparked her interest and she straightened. Up until now, she thought she'd been sitting next to a rock. She'd been beginning to think she was the only one who had been blown away by their kiss. So he wasn't as immovable as he appeared.

She smiled. ''For someone who claims to be so carefree, you sure are in a hurry.''

He stared straight ahead, one hand on the wheel. The other he rested casually on the stick shift. ''I'm not the one in a hurry.''

''What? Surely you're not referring to me.''

He arched a brow at her, then returned his attention to the road.

She waited for his comment. He said nothing. She narrowed her eyes at him. ''What's that look supposed to mean?''

His lips curved in a slow, smug grin that implied he knew that she knew what he was thinking. Except she didn't.

''You really think I'm in a hurry to get to Branson?'' This didn't make any sense. Unless he thought she was anxious to get the trip over with.

''Nope.''

She waited, but apparently that's all he planned on saying. *Men.* ''Gee, I could have stayed home and talked to my Boston fern.''

He chuckled. It was the first normal sound out of him since the kiss. ''No mystery. It's just that you're the one who seems to always be in a hurry.''

''Because I wanted the house finished on time?''

She blinked when she realized she'd used the past

tense. Unsure whether he noticed, she watched him adjust his collar. He had switched shirts while she'd run home to make a couple of phone calls and drop off her car. When he'd arrived to pick her up, he'd not only changed to a light blue Polo shirt but had also put on a pair of khaki slacks. He looked nice but she much preferred him in jeans.

"You still do, don't you?" he asked after an odd silence. Obviously he'd caught her slip.

She sighed. "Yes." Despite her best effort, not a whole lot of conviction stood behind the word.

He readjusted his collar, then tapped a nervous rhythm on the wheel.

The blood suddenly drained from her face. Surely he didn't think that he had anything to do with...

"What else do you think I'm in such a hurry about?" she asked, not sure she knew where she was going with this line of questioning. But she had to get him talking, find out what he was thinking.

"It was a joke, okay? You took a dig. I teased back."

"You think I'm rushing this wedding, don't you?"

His jaw tightened. "I'm not going to talk about your marriage, Kelly."

She almost reminded him that he hadn't minded kissing an engaged woman, but she stopped herself just in time. The remark would have been unkind to both of them. She stared miserably out the window.

"Gary told you I rushed things, didn't he?" she finally asked softly.

"Ask him."

She would if she ever saw Gary. But it seemed that ever since they'd decided to get married, he'd made more and more business trips out of town. Biting down on her lip, she averted her face by focusing on the red wildflowers they passed. She was lying to herself again. She wouldn't have asked Gary because she hadn't been prepared for the answer. Was she now?

"Hey."

She felt something brush her wrist and she turned toward John. He withdrew the hand he'd briefly laid on her forearm, and said, "I know you're feeling guilty. I'm feeling like hell myself. But how about we try and salvage the day?"

She offered him a weak smile. She wasn't feeling nearly as guilty as she should. More disoriented. Like her entire world was coming apart at the seams. Gee, no big deal. She slumped in her seat.

"Are we on?" he asked, darting her a concerned look.

She should tell him that she knew Gary had been in town when he said he hadn't. That he'd been crying on John's shoulder because he felt Kelly was rushing him. She knew Gary too well. And the more rationally she thought about it, the more likely the scenario seemed.

"Sure," she said, trying for a better smile. "We'll have a great time in Branson." There was no point in saying anything to John, she decided. As much as she'd like to assuage some of his guilt, Gary was the person with whom she needed to talk. She'd waited too long as it was.

"Okay," he said, "then let's start by changing the subject."

"I'll discuss anything but politics."

"Smart lady," he said, laughing.

Yeah, real smart. "Or whether Jimmy Bartlett will finally put Tommie Nell out of her misery," she joked, trying to get in a better mood. But when he gave her a confused look, she remembered that he didn't know about the couple's longtime relationship.

Just as well. She was an idiot for bringing up anything that had to do with marriage. Sighing, she gave him an apologetic shrug. "Sorry, local joke."

He groaned. "I definitely remember Tommie Nell."

They both laughed, then lapsed into another silence.

After a couple of minutes, he said, "By the way, did you talk to your friend, Ona Mae, when you stopped at home?"

Good. Another crazy but safe topic. She shook her head. "There is no such thing as a short story when it comes to Ona Mae. I figured we'd better save it for when we get back."

"Just as well. I remembered something else you might want to mention to her that should put her mind to rest."

Kelly smiled, pleased that he was taking this matter with Auntie Om seriously. She really was a sweet lady and any time Kelly could lay her fears at rest, she did. And she appreciated John's cooperation, especially since they had a little talk and he now knew that Kelly had not had a nervous breakdown and really did not believe in aliens or in the existence of Bost.

"What's that?" she asked, beginning to believe the day was salvageable after all.

"I know why she might have thought Gary was in town last week."

The smile wavered on Kelly's lips. "What do you mean?"

"His car," he said. "Tom had it."

"Tom?"

"Yeah." He glanced over at her and flashed a smile. "The guy you introduced me to at the diner. Remember?"

"Go on."

A strange look registered across his face before he redirected his attention to a piece of particularly windy road ahead of them, and she realized her voice had cracked.

"Something was wrong with Gary's transmission and Tom swapped cars with him so he could have a look at it."

"How do you know?" she asked, feeling a sudden eerie calm. Probably shock.

"Are you okay?" He shot her a worried look.

"Fine. How do you know about the car?"

"Because Tom drove it over to my place one evening when he came to look at my Jeep."

She pressed cold fingers to the knot forming in her stomach. So Gary really had been out of town and not spilling his guts to John?

"Are you sure you're okay?" he asked.

She shook her head. "Pull over. I think I'm going to be sick."

Chapter Fourteen

John waited for several minutes to give Kelly some privacy. He felt a little ill himself, wondering what was wrong with her. She'd suddenly turned so deathly white his own gut cramped in reaction.

Maybe she was just carsick. The road had twisted brutally a couple of times, and he may have been driving too fast. His mind had been too busy racing in several directions.

Not able to wait another agonizing second, he strode around the rear of the car and immediately saw her hunched over, her hands on her knees, staring at the tall grass ten feet off the road.

As he got closer he heard her mumble, "It doesn't matter. Nothing's changed."

"Kelly?"

She instantly straightened and looked at him with wide frightened eyes. She was probably embarrassed. He hated her feeling that way with him, and opened up his arms to her.

She slowly raised her arms, too, but wrapped them around herself and turned away from him. Before she did, he noticed that her coloring hadn't improved much.

"Kelly? Are you feeling any better?"

"I didn't puke."

Her defensive tone made him smile a little as he stared at her back. "You probably would have felt better if you had."

"Go away."

He reared back his head. Was she upset with him? "You don't need to be embarrassed. It's only me."

She groaned, and kept her face averted, her arms wrapped so tightly around herself that her knuckles were turning white.

John started to take another step toward her, then stopped. He liked being left alone when he was sick. He hated anyone fussing over him. Eyeing her slumped shoulders, a bolt of helplessness jolted him, promptly sparking a flare of irritation. "Did I do something?"

Starting to straighten again, she sighed loudly. Then, shaking her head, she slowly faced him. "It's not you. It's—" She cut herself off and just kept shaking her head.

John was a decisive, take-charge person. It tweaked his pride that he had absolutely no idea what to do or say at the moment. "Why don't you get out of the sun? It can't be helping," he said, and was annoyed to hear the gruffness in his voice.

Slowly she walked toward him, her arms beginning to loosen at her waist. "We'll get to Branson before long. A glass of water will help."

"Maybe we shouldn't head off so soon. I'd think the motion would set you off again."

Her smile was sad. "I'll be fine."

John didn't know where the anger was coming from, but he was amazed to find himself struggling to keep his temper in check. It made no sense. He had nothing to be angry about. Except at himself for maybe driving too fast or carelessly because he'd been too preoccupied.

But that knowledge didn't stop the slow burn starting to singe his raw nerves, making his jaw clench, his hands curl into fists.

She stepped wrong and lost her footing for a moment. His hand shot out to support her but she was just out of reach, and in the next second, she righted herself. Without his help.

In that instant, he knew what was getting under his skin.

Her.

And the fact that she was in pain, and he couldn't seem to comfort her.

It was a new experience for him. Although he hated seeing anyone in distress and he considered himself a fairly sympathetic person, this feeling was much more intense than anything he'd ever encountered before. It started in the pit of his stomach and gained momentum as it reached his chest. He swore that, as inconceivable as it seemed, even his heart hurt. Experiencing the pain firsthand couldn't have been any more agonizing for him. If he could trade places with her, he gladly would.

He knew he couldn't, but he wasn't going to let her push him away. He held out his hand again. When she started to ignore it, he cupped her elbow and walked her to the passenger door.

"I'm okay. Honest." She gave him a weak smile. A little color started to return to her cheeks.

"Did you eat anything before you left your house?"

She shook her head, a rusty-sounding chuckle spilling from her dry pale lips. "But I'm not contagious. Don't worry."

"I'm damn worried. Not because I think you're contagious." He pulled her gently to him, tucking her head under his chin. Holding her close reassured him that she was okay, that she wasn't going to break. She looked too fragile right now. Not at all like the Kelly he'd come to...

A vicious curse breached his lips, startling her, shocking him.

"John?" Her cheek left his chest and she tilted her head back to look at him, her eyes growing round with alarm.

He massaged her nape and urged her to lay her head back on his shoulder. "I'm sorry," he said quietly. "I just remembered an important call I was supposed to make."

Feeling the tension in her body, he tried once again to get her to relax against him, but it was too late. He'd blown it. She was pulling away. He let her go. Not because he wanted to, but because he had no right to keep her.

"I'm afraid you'll have to wait until we get to Branson," she said, running a hand through her tousled hair. "I don't think there are any rest stops or phone booths along the way."

"Maybe we should skip Branson and turn around

now," he said, and pushed back a thick swatch of hair that had fallen across her cheek.

She jerked and angled away from him. "That wouldn't make sense. We're so close. Anyway, I'm fine."

"It's me, isn't it?" John buried his hands in his pocket so he wouldn't touch her again. "I said or did something wrong."

There was no hesitation in the brisk shake of her head. A sad smile lifted one side of her mouth. "It has nothing to do with you. Honest."

Only half believing her, he watched her gaze into the wooded landscape, a melancholy expression shadowing her face. The wind had picked up and a gentle breeze finished the job of escorting the wispy stray tendrils off her cheeks.

And without warning that overwhelming powerlessness descended upon him again, triggering his temper.

"If you're going to be moody the rest of the afternoon, I'd just as soon turn back now," he said, and stooped down to pick up a rock. He sailed it through the trees.

Leaves rustled. Obviously frightened, a squirrel scampered up a gnarled sycamore tree, chattering above the symphony of chirping birds.

She arched a brow in John's direction. "Feel better?"

Sheepish was more like it. He bent to pick up another rock. "I'm not the one with a problem."

"You're right." She clasped her hands together and watched him toss the rock in the air, catch it, then repeat the process. "I'm not being any fun at all. I'm sorry."

Great. Now he felt like a bigger jerk. "If you don't feel well, you don't feel well. But I don't think you're being up-front with me. There's something else going on here."

Kelly shivered as she watched him toss the rock into the air again. He was using the exercise to not look at her. Which was a good thing. She didn't want him to see the vulnerability in her face.

She wasn't sure she liked this unnerving ability he had to see past her first defense. As close as she was to Ellie and Lana and Gary, none of them challenged her moods like John did. That he managed to see beyond her bluster was both annoying and endearing.

Folding her arms across her chest, she refocused her attention on a bluebird picking at a dead Dogwood branch. "And if I admit that you're right, that there is something else going on here, will you leave it alone?"

He hesitated for a couple of long minutes, making her want to sneak a peek at him, but she stood firm and continued to watch the bird's progress.

"If that's what you want me to do," he finally said, so quietly she had to look at him this time.

He was watching her, the rock fisted in his hand. It was amazing how he could look angry and anxious at the same time.

With sudden and eerie clarity, she understood him. He felt helpless, just as she always did right before her temper got the better of her. And as she'd learned to do over the years, John was struggling for control.

She gave him a weak but encouraging smile. "I've

come to some realizations today,'' she said, then stared down at his leather deck shoes.

She didn't want him guessing what the problem was, and if he already had, she didn't want him finding confirmation in her eyes. And heaven help her, she didn't want to see any pity in his.

"These, uh, realizations have given me a lot to think about," she continued, hastily adding, "but they have nothing to do with you."

"Nothing?" he asked and she felt his warm, slightly callused hand wrapped around her forearm. He tugged until she looked up at him.

The sun was hitting him in the face and he had to squint to look at her. Tiny lines radiated from the corners of his eyes—the same lines that appeared when he smiled or laughed. John did that often. Gary didn't. He used to, but it seemed as if Kelly didn't make him very happy anymore.

Sighing with disgust, she broke away from John. She didn't have to look for pity in his face. She was storing a healthy enough supply of her own so tight in her chest that she was ready to explode. She couldn't remember a time when she didn't know she was going to marry Gary. Everyone in Bachelor Falls had expected it.

Not Ellie or Lana or Ona Mae, a small voice reminded her.

Kelly swallowed hard and slanted John a fleeting look. He must have sensed her need for silence and privacy because he leaned against the Jeep and stared off toward an ancient sycamore crowding several smaller trees.

Her faltering relationship with Gary really did have

nothing to do with John. How many times had she and Ellie and Lana privately criticized other girls in high school who jumped from one boy to the next? Kelly had no intention of doing that.

She stole a furtive look at the admirable way he filled out his Polo shirt. His tanned forearms were corded and muscled in just the right places, and she recalled in vivid detail how it felt for them to be wrapped around her body.

Her pulse sped up, and under the hot June sun, goose bumps appeared on her flesh. Taking a deep, calming breath, she looked away. In a sense he was partly responsible for her awakening. He'd been a catalyst. One who'd taught her about chemistry. And now she wasn't ready to live the rest of her life without tingling again.

But no, Kelly wasn't looking for a replacement.

She silently laughed at herself. Even if she were, John wasn't a suitable candidate. He was still sowing his wild oats, content doing short-term jobs and living in rented cabins while he saw the country. As smart and intuitive and sexy as he was, he was still basically a free spirit.

He didn't live in a commune or have long hair or live hand-to-mouth, but he was no different from the slew of men who had traipsed through her mother's house. Men whose ambitions were no loftier than a warm bed and even warmer body.

Okay, maybe she was being harsh in her assessment, she admitted as she slid him another look. He wasn't irresponsible; creditors weren't breathing down his neck. If they had been, she thought wryly, all of Bachelor Falls would know about it by now.

But his life-style pushed an emotional button she couldn't seem to get past.

Which was probably just as well.

"I'm ready to get started again," she said as brightly as she was able. She still had a lot of thinking to do, but she certainly wasn't going to resolve anything standing here on the side of the road.

He nodded, but remained silent while she walked around him and slipped into the Jeep. John climbed into the driver's seat. He paused, his fingers hovering over the keys he'd left in the ignition. "I want to help," he said without looking at her. "But I don't know how."

The words were hard for him to say. She could tell by the rigid way he held himself, by the stilted quality of his voice. His ready display of vulnerability touched her, and she was tempted to confide in him.

Kelly laid a hand on his arm. A muscle jumped at her touch. "You are helping. You—" She stopped herself. She couldn't do it. Telling him anything more would be unfair to Gary. He needed to be the first to hear what she had to say about their future. "You could buy me lunch," she said.

He turned the key in the ignition, a slow smile curving his mouth. "Okay." Without even a glance in her direction, he checked the side mirror for any unlikely traffic behind them, then pulled the Jeep onto the highway. "But no diet today, right?"

"I wouldn't even think of it."

"Good," he said, his grin broadening.

Her smile was a little more rueful. It seemed as though she wouldn't need to fit into Sunshine's wedding dress, after all.

JOHN NODDED to the waitress's offer to refill his coffee, then turned back to watching Kelly attack her hot fudge sundae.

She hadn't been kidding about ignoring her diet. Although she hadn't finished her club sandwich, she'd done a respectable job of wolfing down her fries and cherry coke. When she ordered extra whipped cream and a side of caramel sauce for her sundae, he hadn't been able to hold back a chuckle.

Fortunately his slip hadn't offended her. She'd simply warned him to order his own dessert because she wasn't sharing.

"What are you looking at?" she asked over the top of the demolished ice cream. She took a self-conscious look around the nearly empty restaurant, then dipped her spoon into the whipped topping. When he didn't answer, she licked the creamy foam off the spoon with slow but joyful relish.

He had to hand it to her. She made eating an art form. Smiling, he sipped his coffee.

"Staring at me won't help. I told you I never share sundaes." She fished out the cherry with her thumb and forefinger, then popped it into her mouth. "And I don't feel one bit guilty, either."

Plowing the spoon through the caramel, she scooped it up and drizzled the sauce over the melting ice cream, then swirled it with the fudge. It looked pretty disgusting. No way he'd have a bite even if she paid...

Her eyes closed briefly and her tongue swept a streak of sauce off her lower lip. Ecstasy spread across her face and her shoulders did that little shimmy number.

Okay, so he could think of a couple of ways she could get him to take a bite.

"What's going on in that evil little mind of yours?" she asked with narrowed eyes, nearly causing him to choke on his coffee. She slid the sundae closer to her. "You're so obvious. It's written all over your face."

"It is?" He tried not to laugh. She had no idea what was racing through his mind. If she did, she'd share the sundae, all right. She'd dump it in the middle of his lap.

After eyeing him with dwindling suspicion for another moment, she returned her full attention to carefully threading the caramel through the fudge. He'd bet his last dollar she'd eat the entire thing. And then she'd probably be sick again.

Although he suspected her earlier attack had been the result of something emotional rather than physical. The more he thought about it, the more he reviewed the day's events in his mind, the more convinced he was that Kelly had finally come to the same realization Gary had come to several weeks ago.

She wouldn't have kissed John if she hadn't.

He took too big a sip of coffee and burned his mouth.

Inwardly he cursed his stupidity. He'd promised himself he'd stay out of their affairs. Gary had talked too much. Kelly had been too...unexpected. And now John felt as though he was in the middle somehow.

He'd had no business kissing her. He wasn't a kid who couldn't control his hormones. Yet even now, watching her lick the stubborn fudge from the corners of her mouth, his body tightened with need.

Snorting soundlessly with self-disgust, he pushed the mug aside and reached into his pocket. "We'd better get a move on if we want to pick up that molding. You still have to look at samples."

The spoon went limp in her hand and she slowly set it down, then sank back against her seat. She removed the napkin from her lap and brought it to her lips. After a couple of slow deliberate dabs, she laid the white paper down beside her plate and raised a hesitant gaze to his. "I was thinking maybe we should hold off on buying any more molding."

His hand clenched the wad of bills he'd pulled out of his pocket until his fingers cramped. Quickly he transferred his gaze from hers to the check sitting near the edge of the table. Picking it up, he studied it.

She probably expected him to ask why her change of heart. Except he already knew the answer. Then again, maybe she was hoping he wouldn't ask. And maybe he was wrong altogether.

"John?" She tried to pluck the check from his hand. "Let me get that."

Glancing up at her anxious face, he realized he'd been staring too long. "I got it," he said, and threw down a handful of bills.

Her eyes drew to the money and widened. "I know I didn't eat *that* much."

He frowned, then fished two twenties out of the crumpled pile and stuffed them back in his pocket. "Why did you change your mind about the molding?"

She started at the sudden question, then slumped and exhaled loudly. "I don't know that I have. I just don't want to get it today."

Her eyes wouldn't meet his and he knew she was lying. "Are you feeling ill again?"

She laughed and sent a wry look at the ravished sundae. A mere chocolaty puddle remained. "If I were, I'd deserve it. But no, I'm fine. Are you sure I can't pick up that check?"

"I think I can afford it."

She frowned at his sarcastic tone. "I wasn't implying you couldn't."

He nodded an apology. Normally he wasn't so touchy. It was that helpless feeling again, starting to close in. He wanted her to talk to him, to confirm what he figured he already knew. "If you don't want to go look at molding samples, what did you want to do? Shop? Check out a concert? I'm at your mercy."

Her gaze lowering, she picked at the corner of her napkin until it began to shred. "You won't like it."

"Try me."

"I want to go back to Bachelor Falls."

He wasn't surprised. "Something I said?"

"Oh, no." She looked up. "It's not you."

"Yeah, so you've told me."

Her mouth turned down at the corners and her eyes looked so sad that he felt like a heel for making the crack.

"Hey, no big deal," he said, reaching across the table and squeezing her cold hand. Then he started to slide out of the booth, stopped and inclined his head toward the kitchen door. "You want to order something for the road?"

She blinked in openmouthed indignation, then started to slide out of her seat, too. "All right, buster.

Very funny. But you didn't do that bad a job on your double bacon cheeseburger and steak fries.''

He laughed. ''Hey, I'm a growing boy.''

Her gaze promptly dropped to his chest and meandered down to his belly. Hell, he wished she'd quit looking at him like that. His only consolation was that she'd die of humiliation if she knew how transparent her expression was. But even that knowledge didn't help much.

Yeah, he was a growing boy, all right. He shifted against the sudden snug fit of his slacks. Oh, man, how was he supposed to stand now?

She cleared her throat. ''I'm going to stop in the ladies' room.''

''Good idea,'' he said, and when she gave him a funny look, he added, ''I'm going to do the same. Go to the men's room, that is.''

''Of course.'' Her lips started to curve as she turned and headed toward the back of the restaurant.

John waited until she was out of sight. About the same time, things down south started calming down and he gingerly stood. It was already late afternoon and only two other tables were occupied. Even the lone waitress had disappeared through the kitchen door.

After stopping to pick up a peppermint at the cash register, he strode outside and leaned against his Jeep, glad for the break in the clouds and for the burning sun soaking into his skin. It wasn't as though he wasn't hot enough already, but somehow the warm rays always soothed his spirit.

One of the things he liked most about the states he'd visited was the abundance of sunshine. That was one of the main reasons he'd chosen to return to carpentry after he'd retired. So that he could partially work outside. Back in his small hometown near London, fog and rain dominated the weather. By the time he'd left at fifteen, he still hadn't gotten used to the long stretches of dreary sunless days.

Right now, out here with the sun beating down on his head and shoulders, things didn't seem so bad. As much as he'd love to spend the time alone with Kelly, she was right to want to return to Bachelor Falls.

For one thing, if he was correct in his assumptions, there was a lot she needed to get off her chest with Gary, who was returning this evening. And the sooner she did that, the better off she'd feel.

Secondly, he had his own selfish reasons. John was having trouble keeping his hands off her. That bothered him on a couple of different levels. He'd always been an honorable man. But lately, his thoughts held about as much integrity as a con artist ripping off lonely widows.

Until Kelly declared otherwise, she was still engaged to another man. And no matter what, he was determined to abide by that fact.

She emerged from the restaurant, the sun picking up the reddish gold highlights in her hair, and his heart squirmed in his chest.

"Ready?" He quickly climbed into the Jeep. As far as he was concerned, the sooner they got back the better.

"Ready," she confirmed and slipped in beside him.

He pushed the key into the ignition and turned it. The engine made a funny sound, sputtered and died. He tried again. And received the same result.

"I thought Tom fixed it," she said, her eyes widening.

He turned the key several more times until he smelled gas. Abandoning his efforts, he sunk back in a pool of dread, then hit the wheel with the heel of his hand.

Chapter Fifteen

"You want two rooms?" the front desk clerk asked, her gaze glued to the computer screen as she typed in some information.

"Two," John quickly assured her. So quickly, in fact, that Kelly slid him a curious sidelong look.

She didn't know why he was so nervous. He'd even offered to rent a car to drive back to Bachelor Falls, which was absurd since in the past two hours it had started to rain like the dickens, and his Jeep was going to be fixed the first thing tomorrow morning anyway.

Without looking up, the clerk frowned at the computer screen. "I have only one left. We're pretty full today."

"Fine. We'll try someplace else."

Kelly gave him a bland look the same time the pretty blond woman flashed them an apologetic smile. "I don't think you'll have much luck. Several tour groups that were supposed to check out got stranded by the rain. All the other hotels are having the same problem."

No kidding. This was their third hotel and they were already both dripping wet. If he didn't grab that one room while he could, Kelly was going to strangle him.

She sighed softly and tried not to let her feelings get hurt. She didn't understand him. The way he was acting all of a sudden reminded her of the boys in third grade who'd lived in fear of getting girl cooties. Well, she had no intention of spreading her cooties around.

She opened her mouth to tell him so, when the young woman behind the desk perked up. "Wait a minute. Here we go. I found another room. But I'm afraid it's really small and in the process of being wallpapered, plus it's at the opposite end of the building from the other one."

"We'll take them both." John whipped out his credit card.

"I'm paying for my own room," Kelly said, and fumbled with her wallet.

He covered her hand with his to stop her. Before she could say anything, he snatched his back as if he'd been singed and dragged his palm down his wet khakis. "Let me get it, Kelly. This is my fault."

She had a smart retort on the tip of her tongue. Something about her cooties not being contagious, but as soon as her attention drew to the front of his soaked slacks, the remark shriveled and dissolved in her mouth.

Holy smoke. Her gaze flew to his face. "Two rooms. Good idea."

No wonder he was acting so peculiar.

She wished she hadn't seen the way his arousal pushed against the wet fabric. She really did.

Nevertheless, her gaze wandered helplessly downward again. A brief enough peek shouldn't count against her, she figured. Finding what she was looking for, she shivered with awareness.

"We'll get you warm and dry in no time," he said, and started to slip an arm around her. He stopped, obviously thinking better of that move, and let his arm drop to his side. Flashing Kelly a tentative smile, he signed the credit card voucher the clerk handed him.

"Here, this is for my room," Kelly said, and pushed her Visa across the counter.

John started to protest but the clerk had already accepted the charge plate and began processing it.

Kelly drummed her fingers on the counter and waited. Someone opened the door behind them and a rush of cold damp air swooshed into the lobby, sending a chill up her spine.

She turned to find a young couple laughing and wiping the rain off each other's faces. She smiled at them, an odd sadness tugging inexplicably at her, then glanced at John.

He paid them no attention. Impatience bracketed his mouth as he angled his wrist and studied his watch. He was pretty thoroughly soaked, much more than she was. It hadn't escaped her notice that he'd done his best to shield her from the rain whenever possible. He had to be freezing.

"Go on up." She nudged him with her elbow to get his attention. "You don't have to wait for me. We're on opposite sides of the building anyway."

"Right." He nodded absently. "Here's my room number," he said, showing her his key. "Call me later if you want to have dinner."

He didn't hesitate to head for the elevator, and it hardly took a triple-digit IQ to see he couldn't wait to get rid of her. Ordinarily Kelly might have been insulted, but understanding his haste, she merely smiled.

John punched the lit elevator button for the third time. He needed to get to the safety of his room and take a long cold shower. The elevator dinged just as he spotted the staircase.

He paused for a moment. The exercise would probably do his overly tense body some good. Except the elevator would get him to his room quicker. When the doors eased open, he hurried into the car and punched the sixth-floor button twice.

How could this happen? If this wasn't the worst possible time for his Jeep to break down, he didn't know when would be. He was going to wring Tom's neck. The guy had sworn up and down he'd fixed the problem.

As soon as John stuck his key in the door, it occurred to him what he'd done. Without finding out who had gotten which room, he'd flown out of the lobby as though he'd been set on fire. Which, in a way, he had.

He opened the door and knew right away that he'd left Kelly with the crummy room. The decor in this one was a pleasant mix of mauve and blue. A king-size bed faced expansive glass windows. Snorting, he shook his head. It wasn't as if he hadn't done less gentlemanly things today.

After throwing the key on the dresser, he pulled off his wet shirt, wrung it out, then hung it over a pole in the tub. He'd give her time to settle in, then he'd call and offer to switch rooms. At least they didn't have any luggage to worry about. It wouldn't be a hassle to trade.

But he didn't want to see her yet. They needed a short time-out. Time enough for him to get his head screwed back on straight. He'd spent part of the afternoon sweating it, wondering if they were going to end up sharing a room. The other part he'd spent uneasily aroused, hoping they would. Stupid. Very stupid.

After dropping his soggy khakis, he kicked them to the side and checked behind the bathroom door for a robe. Finding none, he pulled a large fluffy white towel off the rack and draped it around his waist, then went to pick up his wet pants.

There wasn't much left to do but take a nap while his clothes dried a little. Had either of them been thinking clearly, they could have picked up something to wear after settling things with the slow-as-molasses mechanic and before they'd checked in. Now he wasn't inclined to go tramping through the rain again.

Not that he thought he'd get any sleep. Too much had happened today. Too many emotions had been stirred, not to mention a few randy hormones.

Having hung his pants beside his shirt, he picked up the remote control, aimed it at the television and pressed the on button. He started to sink onto the bed when someone knocked at the door. Muttering a word his foster mother would have swatted him for, he pushed off the mattress and looked out the peephole.

Kelly?

His hand fisted the knob, but he stopped and glanced down at the white towel, his bare legs. He didn't want to put on those wet, soggy clothes again.

Bloody hell. Maybe when she saw that he was half-naked she'd run back to her room where she belonged.

He jerked open the door.

The smile she'd had in place wavered on her lips. She blinked, but carefully kept her eyes level with his. "Hi."

"Yeah?"

The smile vanished. "Can I come in?"

Stupid idea. Very stupid. Stepping aside, he gestured her in with a flourish.

Her smile returned. It was brief, a little timid, as she glided past him. "Wow," she said, looking around, "not bad. The armoire is cherry, isn't it?"

Their rooms couldn't be *that* different. Hotel furnishings were fairly standard issue. He frowned. "Haven't you been to your room yet?"

Giving a brisk shake of her head, she walked toward the bed. She pressed a palm to the mattress, testing it, then spun around and plopped down with a bounce. "I like hotel mattresses. They're always firm."

Her hair and clothes were still wet and water flew everywhere. She noticed the fat drops that had landed on the mauve quilt and briefly covered her mouth with her hand. "Oops. Sorry. The last thing we need is more water around here," she said as she slowly scooted off the bed.

We? Probably an innocent remark, but he still didn't like the sound of that.

"Well..." Clasping her hands together, she roamed the room, checking out the digital alarm, the stationery sitting on the desk, but being careful not to look at him.

Her studied avoidance made him uneasy, and then he remembered he was just wearing the towel. He chuckled to himself. No wonder she was nervous.

"Kelly? What did you want?"

"Dinner," she said without looking at him. "I was wondering what time you wanted to go eat."

"You're not hungry already?" He stepped into her line of vision.

She did something he hadn't seen her do before. She stuck out her lower lip in a pout. "No, but I want to be prepared."

"I'm not criticizing you," he said quickly. "If you're hungry now, we'll go eat. Or you could order room service."

Her gaze slid over his shoulders, lingered on his chest and stopped at his waist, where the towel was secured...in a very loose knot.

He passed a hand over his face and briefly covered his mouth. After blowing a stream of warm air into his palm, he jerked his hand away. "You know, that's probably a good idea. Why don't you go back to your room, get out of those wet clothes, call room service?"

When she didn't budge, he slipped behind her, lightly pressed a hand to the small of her back and guided her toward the door. "Sound good? You can have them bring you up something nice and warm to drink."

Several feet from the door, she stopped. "Why are you trying to get rid of me?"

Dropping his hand, he stepped to the side so that

he could look her in the face. No sense in hedging. "I think the answer is obvious."

Her gaze lowered to his towel. "Oh."

"Now that we understand each other..." He gestured her toward the door.

"We have a problem."

No kidding. It was starting to poke at the towel. His patience gone, he said, "Yes?"

"I don't have a room."

"Of course you do. I saw you pay—" He stopped, frowning, and then comprehension dawned. "It's that much of a pit, huh? Don't worry. I was going to trade with you anyway," he said, starting toward the bathroom. "Give me a minute to change."

She grabbed his arm. "Wait. That's not it."

For a second, he felt off balance. Her nails dug lightly into his skin as she gently squeezed his forearm, and he wasn't sure if it was her touch or the dread in her voice that made him reel slightly off center. "Then what?"

"I mean, I *really* don't have a room." Her hand fell to her side and her gaze shot past him. Staring at the door, she said, "I gave it away."

He shook his head. Obviously moisture had leaked in and short-circuited his hearing or his brain. "Tell me you didn't say what I think you said."

Shrugging, she turned toward the window, and presenting him her back, she folded her arms across her chest. "I knew you were going to act this way. If you don't want to share your room with me, fine."

About to point out what a nutcase she was for even considering such a ridiculous idea, he jerked a frustrated hand into the air and the towel started to slip from his waist. Hastily he pulled back his hand to retie the knot.

Apparently his interrupted response took too long because she slowly angled away from the window and sent a peek over her shoulder at him. She uncrossed her arms and abruptly faced him, her eyes growing wide with indignation. "What do you think you're doing?"

His hands froze on the towel. What did she think...?

Silent laughter rumbled in his chest. His face he kept straight. "I thought this is what you wanted." He undid the knot he'd just retied, then his hand paused. "Isn't that what you came here for?" he asked with the perfect mixture of confusion and innocence.

She swung around to face the window again, and putting her hands along the sill, she leaned toward the glass. "I was trying to be a good Samaritan, you turkey."

He snorted. "What? You feel sorry for me so you're giving me a charity roll?"

"No." She stomped her foot and faced him again. The move was impulsive and he could tell she was sorry she had turned around, but she held her ground by looking him directly in the eyes. "The couple who came in after us. I gave them my room."

"How magnanimous of you," he said dryly, and started retying his towel.

"They're on their honeymoon and they were forced to make this unexpected stop. What else was I supposed to do?" she said, studiously watching him fasten the knot.

"Swell. Now, where are you going to sleep?"

She lifted her chin and her eyes met his. "I'll find a place."

"Right." Absently he scratched his chest and glanced around the room. No couch. The chair provided might be okay if you were just watching the tube for a couple of hours. This was bad. Hell, he'd just have to sleep on the floor. Although merely having her in the same room was going to be a bear. "Okay..."

When he brought his attention back to her face, the longing he found there was nearly his undoing. Kelly slowly lifted her gaze from his chest and met him head-on, her topaz eyes brimming with both fear and excitement. Her tongue ran a quick and unconscious path across her lower lip.

"This isn't going to work," he said quietly when he felt his body spring in response.

"I know," she whispered.

He'd find another room. Or sleep in the Jeep if he had to. "It'll be okay."

"I hope so," she said around a nervous laugh. "I expect it to be a little more than okay."

John frowned at the odd look she gave him. "You're not feeling ill again, are you?"

She gave a quick shake of her head and a faint smile. "I know what I'm doing," she said, and slipped the top button of her blouse out of its hole.

"Whoa." He took a couple of steps toward the bathroom. "I'll be out of your hair in three minutes."

She jerked slightly. "What do you mean?"

He stopped at the bathroom door. A faint burning sensation started to gnaw at his gut. He hoped they'd been talking about the same thing when he said it wouldn't work. But if not...

He took a deep breath. The gnawing persisted like a three-alarm warning. "So that you can have the room."

"I don't want the room." She bit her lip, and her drooping shoulders suddenly straightened. "I want you."

The burning exploded into a volcano of emotions sending the blood surging through his veins like hot lava down the side of a cliff. "Kelly, think about what you're saying."

"I have. Before I even knocked on the door." She broke eye contact and stared down at her hands. Her fingers were twisted together in a tight clasp. "I wanted it to be different. I did."

"It still can be."

"Are you saying you don't want me?" she asked, her gaze instantly raised to his probing one, her eyes darkening with humiliation and pain.

"Kelly..."

He didn't have to finish his protest, denial, whatever feeble obstacle his brain was scrambling to come up with. Because once her gaze flicked lower, there was no hope. Hiding his desire was useless. The damn ineffective towel was starting to look like a sail. And judging by the predatory urge instilled in him by her heated look, an ill wind was blowing his way.

She blinked, a slow saucy grin starting to curve her lips. "If you don't, better tell the rest of you," she said, and took a step toward him.

If she thought she was calling his bluff by advancing, she was in for an even bigger surprise. He fisted the knot at his waist, but he didn't back up. "Kelly, you need to really think about what you're doing here."

Her smile turned a little bittersweet and she stopped, only inches from him. Her head tilted back, her uneven breath reaching his chin, warming his senses and diluting his resolve. "Believe me, I've thought of little else. I know what you're thinking," she said. He was glad one of them did. "But you're not the root of my problem, John, and I'm sure not going to make you the solution."

He frowned, not clear on her meaning. But that was no surprise. His heart was beginning to pound with the voracity of a jackhammer and the blood was gushing through his veins like water breaking through a dam.

God help him, as selfish as it was, he didn't want to analyze what was happening or what she was saying, or if he was doing the right thing. He wanted Kelly too much. Far too much.

Bringing a hand to her face, he was amazed at how steady his fingers remained as he cupped her jaw. "Promise me you won't regret this."

"I won't."

"This will change our relationship forever."

"I know," she whispered, and raised herself on tiptoes.

Her lower lip quivered, and he shut his eyes and pressed his mouth to hers. Any other sign of her nervousness disappeared as she met his kiss with hungry urgency. Her arms quickly came around his neck, and she crushed herself to his chest, her breasts pressing hard against him.

He wanted to see them, feel their bare softness quenching his skin's thirst for her. He'd already seen them many times in his mind. Whenever she'd worn those tight blouses of hers, his helpless imagination had gone berserk.

Reaching for a button, his lips stretched in an automatic curve. Maybe his irresponsible, adolescent imagination had been a good thing, after all. Maybe now he wouldn't totally embarrass himself as soon as he saw her in the flesh.

Kelly felt him smile against her lips, and it confused her. Maybe she was being too bold. Maybe she'd misread the signs and he wasn't as interested in her as she was in him. She pulled back, her legs wobbly, her mind and body both too foggy to prepare herself for what she might find in his expression.

His smile broadened. His fingers never left her button, although he was having trouble unfastening it. She didn't offer to help him though. She was too busy relishing the look of tender desire she saw in his eyes as his gaze moved from her face to his hands back to her face.

"What's that smug smile for?" he asked, the tanned skin crinkling at the corners of his eyes.

"I thought you'd be better at this," she said, briefly glancing down at his hand. His question had caught her off guard, and she immediately regretted the critical-sounding remark. But when her eyes reluctantly met his, she had to hold back the laughter. His midnight blues had narrowed dangerously, no doubt to accommodate his injured, swelling ego.

"Oh, yeah?" His fingers had stilled on the second button. Clamping them tighter, he gave a sudden jerk and buttons flew everywhere. "That's better," he said, pushing her blouse aside.

She jumped, swallowed and struggled against the urge to cross her arms over her chest. "I can't believe you did that," she said. "I don't have any other clothes."

"There's a sewing kit in the desk drawer." His voice was oddly hoarse as his gaze lowered to her chest. "I'll put them back on later."

Oh, Lord, she hoped she had on a decent bra. She sent a furtive glance downward. The pink lacy one. Thank goodness.

She heaved a sigh of relief.

John groaned. His right hand moved from the front of her blouse and the back of his fingers trailed across the tops of her breasts. Ordinarily, she might have squirmed under such close scrutiny, but the rapt look of tenderness and longing on his face assured her, making her feel powerful and beautiful and very much desired.

Wiggling slightly, she let her blouse fall off one shoulder, while John pushed the other side off. Then he swung the freed garment up and sailed it toward a chair.

His fingers moved with swift deftness to the front of her bra clasp, and she quickly said, "Maybe I should do that."

He chuckled, and easily disengaged the silky fabric with everything still intact. Except her breasts. They burst free and she waited for the shyness to hit. It didn't come. Couldn't come. Not with the way John's lips parted, the way his eyes darkened and the sharp way he sucked in a breath.

He touched her so softly that if she hadn't seen the tips of his fingers graze her skin she wasn't sure she would have felt the contact. Her nipples did, and responded in brash swiftness. They pebbled, beckoning him, almost begging him.

Cupping her fullness in his palm, he closed his eyes as if giving himself a moment to learn the feel of her. An incredibly sexy and satisfied expression flitted across his face and as his eyes slowly opened again, Kelly felt liquid heat flow between her thighs.

Excited, impatient, she reached for the knot in his towel.

But he'd already started to lower his head, putting his body slightly out of reach, as he touched his tongue to one fevered nipple.

Pleasure shot through her quicker than a shooting star across a midnight sky. Her knees weakened and she clung to his shoulders. His arm circled her waist, supporting her when she would have sunk to the floor. His thumb wedged into the waistband of her shorts.

She wanted her shorts off, along with his towel. She wanted to stretch out naked beside him on the bed, their bodies touching at every curve. And most of all, she wanted these things because she knew he did, too. John wanted *her*.

Dragging her hands away from his shoulders, she framed his face, holding both sides of his jaw and forcing him to look up. His eyes instantly met hers, their usual clarity glazed by both desire and fear.

"Second thoughts?" he asked, his voice barely serviceable.

She shook her head while her hands returned to his

shoulders, then she slowly backed up, pulling him with her until the bed hit the backs of her legs.

He carefully watched her face as if to detect whether she was having a change of heart. The idea made her smile. As if her heart would listen to anything but sharing itself with this man.

John returned the smile and brushed his lips against hers. "Everything's okay?"

"Everything but my blouse."

His grin widened. "You're not going to let me live that down."

"Maybe. Depends on how good a job you do sewing the buttons back on."

He pushed the hair away from the side of her face and kissed her neck. "Oh, I'll do an excellent job. I guarantee you."

She shivered, not doubting him. A fresh current of anticipation charged through her, the sensation so absurdly physical that when she shifted in reaction, she ended up landing with her bottom on the bed, surprising them both.

Peering up at him, she gave him a weak smile. "Really?" Well, that was brilliant.

He reached for her zipper. "I know how to sew. You'll find that I'm very self-sufficient."

She didn't doubt that either. He was independent and carefree. John didn't need her. He wasn't like Gary.

The sudden reminder of her fiancé made her stiffen a little. Oddly though, it didn't upset her. If she hadn't finally faced the truth, that they were both willing to give up love for security, they would have gotten married as planned. She would have had her house and stability. And Gary would have merely done what everyone in Bachelor Falls had expected of him.

That may have been enough for her last month. It wasn't now. She moved her hips to give John better access to her zipper but his hand had stilled. A cloud of wariness shadowed his face, and she was sorry he'd mistaken her reverie for hesitation.

"Don't get crazy with the zipper, okay?" she whispered. "They aren't as easy to replace as buttons."

A brief smiled touched his lips. "Kelly?"

Her heart ached suddenly at the uncertainty in his eyes. There was no mistaking how much he wanted her, yet he was concerned for her readiness. Or maybe he thought she was going to turn into a clinging vine once they'd made love....

She didn't know how to reassure him that wouldn't happen, that she understood this was going to be a one-shot deal. Well, maybe a couple or three shots. As long as he felt inclined to stay in Bachelor Falls, anyway.

Because as much as he prized his carefree independence, Kelly still craved stability. Even if it meant living a life like Ona Mae—alone, waiting. John had taught her about love and chemistry and made her realize her marriage wouldn't survive without it. Ironically, the discovery would leave her with neither. Except for now, this moment. Because she did love John.

She swallowed back the lump of emotion produced by the undeniable realization and reached for the zipper herself.

He stopped her. "Kelly? I want you. But even more I want you to be sure."

"I am. Trust me."

He did trust her. She could see it in his eyes, but she saw hesitancy lurking there, too. Hoping she understood the source, she reached into her pocket and withdrew the foil packet she'd picked up in the gift shop, then laid it on the nightstand.

A smile touched his eyes before he bent and kissed her, then finished disengaging the zipper. His motions were swift and economical after that, and within seconds his towel joined her shorts and pink panties in a heap on the floor.

His skin was warm and tanned clear down to his waist, with just the right amount of dark hair across his chest. When he hugged her to him, she stroked the well-defined muscles forming his shoulders and back, using her palm to knead and rub until she reached the swell of his firm buttocks.

He pushed her gently back then, and took a puckered ripe nipple into his mouth and suckled until she grew so wet she thought she'd die. In defense, she'd clamped her thighs together, but as soon as his hand began massaging the top of her leg, all her muscles and bones went as limp as a piece of overcooked spaghetti.

John wasted no time in finding her heat. His touch was gentle yet rough, deft yet restrained. But Kelly didn't want restraint. She wanted him inside her. Now.

When she slid her palm down his sex, he shuddered and tried to slow her. But she wouldn't let him. Instead, she opened the foil packet, and rolled the condom onto him. Then, moving into position, she guided him toward her.

Ignoring his last ragged plea for her to wait, she slid onto him. He thrust reflexively into her, stealing her breath, knocking her momentarily senseless and dazed.

For the first time in her life, Kelly felt totally, insanely, frighteningly out of control.

And she wished the feeling would never end.

Chapter Sixteen

Kelly opened her eyes and stared at the digital clock on the nightstand. Hard to believe it was morning already. She rotated a stiff shoulder. It wasn't the only thing that felt achy. Every joint, nook and cranny in her body felt different this morning. *She* felt different, period.

She sighed. It must truly be love. She hadn't even given her missed dinner a fleeting thought.

"Morning," John said, his voice deep and hazy with sleep as he kissed the back of her shoulder. His beard was a little scratchy, just enough to tickle, and she giggled.

"What's so funny?"

She heard the smile in his voice even before she turned around to see it reflected in his eyes. "Your beard tickles."

He looked startled at first, then irritated as he brought a hand to his jaw. "Oh, yeah."

"I'm not complaining," she said, tugging at his hand.

"I picked up a razor in the gift shop. I'll go

shave," he said, starting to roll toward the edge of the bed.

"Right now?"

The disappointment in her voice was plain and he stopped long enough to cup her cheek, kiss the tip of her nose. Then he pulled his head back, giving her a long thoughtful look. "I like you better without so much makeup."

She lifted a self-conscious hand to her cheek. It had been a long time since anyone saw her nearly bare-faced. "What? You don't like the Marilyn Monroe look?" she asked with a small, self-deprecating grin.

He laughed and hugged her. "Is that what the tight blouses and heavy makeup is all about?"

Kelly made a face. "The makeup is because Sunshine wouldn't let me wear any, and the tight blouses are because of too much chocolate. But that isn't a problem anymore." She lifted her chin. "I lost seven pounds in the past two weeks."

"I like the tight blouses better," he said, and nuzzled her neck while curling his arm around her and helping himself to a handful of her fanny.

"Hey." Self-conscious again, she squirmed. "Your beard is tickling," she lied.

He froze. "I'll go shave right now."

When he started to pull away, she was immediately sorry she'd told the fib. "Don't." She flipped over and tugged on his arm. "We'll have to get up and pick up the car in a couple of hours. Let's just…you know…stay in bed until we have to get up."

He had one leg out of the bed, causing the sheet to fall away from his naked body, and she was pleased to see he was already hard. Although it didn't surprise her. They had made love several times during the night and he'd always been ready.

His gaze followed hers, and he chuckled. "It'll only take me a minute to shave," he said, his hand once again finding his jaw, covering it, almost as though he was trying to hide it. "But you're making it awfully hard."

Her grin widened, her gaze lowered purposefully.

"Damn it," he said, and slid back into bed.

"I think it's very noble of you to worry about me," she said, showering several light kisses along his jaw, "but I think you'll find I'm not as sensitive as you might think."

"Uh-huh." He pinned her arms down on either side of her head and pressed three long hot kisses down her neck to her collarbone.

She shivered with delight, briefly closing her eyes. As she opened them again and looked at him in this new angle and light, she blinked and said, "Your beard. It's red."

His face fell. "That does it. I'm shaving right now."

Leaning back, he let go of her arms. Using the element of surprise as her weapon, she grabbed him around the waist and wrestled him down, finally straddling him and pinning his arms to his sides.

"Not so fast," she said with a pretend scowl.

One side of his mouth lifted in a lopsided smile. "Now that you have me, what are you going to do with me?"

Something stirred beneath her. It was pretty obvious what he wanted her to do to him. She held back a smile. "Get some answers. Now, tell me why you're touchy about this beard of yours."

His grin disappeared and he sighed with annoyance. "It's red."

"So?" She eyed it closer. It wasn't truly red. It just had a reddish cast.

"I have dark hair. It's not supposed to be red."

"And it irritates you." She tilted her head to the side, thinking about how he was always clean shaven no matter what time of day it was.

"Gee, Sherlock, you're wasting your talents as a bookkeeper."

She laughed. "It's funny to see you so touchy... about anything."

His eyebrows drew together. "Look, from now on I don't mention your makeup, you don't mention my beard."

He was genuinely edgy about this particular issue and she did her best not to let her amusement show. It wasn't terribly hard to accomplish that when the thought struck her that there was so much they didn't know about each other. Even more they'd never discover.

She pushed the crippling thought aside. "Deal—*if* you throw in never to mention the word *diet* either."

"Not for as long as I live," he said, the smile returning to his lips as he easily extricated his wrists from her hold.

In one swift movement, she was flat on her back and he was stretched out above her. The breath fled her lungs in a swoosh and she sputtered in surprise. He stopped the sound with a long sweet kiss.

Kelly relaxed against the pillows and fought off the

lingering sadness. He didn't have to worry about their deal for as long as he lived. Just until the end of summer. When they said goodbye.

"ALMOST THERE and we haven't broken down yet." John gave her a smug wink, then reached across the seat to squeeze her thigh.

She jerked a hair out of reach. The move was subtle, probably just reflexive, but it wasn't the first time he'd noticed her pulling away from him since leaving Branson.

"Don't get too cocky," she said. "We're not there yet and I still say old Oscar looked pretty hungover to me. I just may win the bet yet."

He laughed. The paunchy, ruddy-faced mechanic had grumbled that he'd worked on the Jeep half the night. Probably to justify the outrageous bill he'd presented to John. But Kelly insisted the guy had spent the night drinking, which made her wary of driving the Jeep home.

John hoped it was because she simply didn't want to go back to Bachelor Falls, that she wanted an excuse to stay in their own little world suspended above reality. But the truth was, she didn't want to face Gary. John didn't blame her. The idea of seeing Gary made him a little queasy, too.

It didn't matter that John knew for a fact Gary would be relieved to have the wedding called off. In a town like Bachelor Falls, fingers always pointed. And if someone found out that either of them had been out of town all night and put two and two together...

Well, no matter what, it was going to be uncomfortable for Kelly for a while. For John, too, although he didn't care about that. He didn't have to live there. In fact, maybe it would be kinder to Kelly if he left now. After all, she probably wasn't in such a rush to get her house finished anymore.

The thought of leaving her really did make him feel sick. So why did he have to leave? He liked Bachelor Falls, and there was probably enough work for him in the tricounty area. Glancing over at her sullen profile, he reached out a hand, hoping she wouldn't flinch. He had to touch her.

As soon as his hand covered hers, she smiled and turned her palm up until it pressed against his, then she entwined their fingers. His heart picked up speed. There was hope for them. He felt it in the weight of her smile, the warmth of her skin, her pulse keeping time with his. He just had to be patient.

For the next fifteen minutes, they drove in a comfortably tacit silence until they saw a sign indicating they were approaching the falls.

She sighed. "Looks like you'll win the bet. We should get to town within five minutes." Frowning, she added, "What was the wager, anyway? We didn't settle on anything."

He slid a lascivious look her way before facing the road, and grinning. "Well, let's see…"

She let go of his hand. Her nervous laughter filled the Jeep, and put a knot in his belly. "I don't know about that."

He didn't say anything. Kelly liked to be in control. This was her town, her future, her call. Patience. If they had any chance at all, he'd have to be patient.

"Hey," he said, deciding it was time to change the

subject. "We haven't decided what we're going to tell Ona Mae. Unless you want to pretend we were both abducted by aliens last night."

As soon as the words were out of his mouth he wanted to shoot himself. The last thing she needed was a reminder that they might be in for some grilling. But Kelly didn't seem upset. She laughed until tears filled her eyes.

"Are you okay?" he asked, his gaze darting from her to the road, then back to her.

Kelly shook her head at first, then nodded. "I'm fine," she said, and it was mostly the truth. She swallowed the last of her laughter. She was still tired from staying up most of the night and felt a tinge of hysteria hovering at the edge of her sanity. She had a big day ahead of her. Not a very pleasant one, either. "I was just picturing us insisting we were abducted. The whole town would go absolutely nuts."

He half snorted, half sighed. "I don't suppose if anyone noticed your absence they'd keep their mouths shut."

She gave him a dry look. "In Bachelor Falls? But don't worry about it. I'm not."

He didn't believe her.

"I'm really not," she insisted, tugging at his arm until he gave her one of his hands. "People don't know you or your routine. They probably didn't even know you were out of town. I just want to get to Gary first."

He nodded. "I wish I could make things better for you."

"You already have."

He gave her a sharp look and the car swerved a

little. That was probably why he snatched back his hand and placed it on the wheel, she told herself as she clasped her own hands together on her lap.

She took a deep breath. "The only thing I meant by that is I'm glad I had the time to think. Getting away was a good idea."

When he remained silent, anger coiled like a snake in her stomach. He didn't have a damn thing to worry about. It wasn't as if she was going to try and trap him or anything. He was totally unsuitable. Definitely not husband material. She wanted someone who knew boundaries, and who brought home a steady paycheck. Someone who would grow roots.

"Kelly?"

As soon as he called her out of her reverie, and she looked into his earnest blue eyes, her anger died. She had no right to be upset with him. He'd promised her nothing. But she knew too that she was angrier with herself. She wanted something she couldn't have.

"Kelly?" He pulled the Jeep over to the side of the road and let it idle. "You look so sad. Talk to me."

"I still don't know what to tell Ona Mae," she blurted out. It was all she could think to say.

He shrugged. "Let's tell her the truth."

"That we spent the night together in Branson?"

He laughed. "No. I meant about my government checks. I'm sure that's what has her in an uproar."

She stared at him, confused. "Our government? I mean, as in Uncle Sam?" He straightened, an odd look crossing his face, and knowing that she'd somehow offended him, she laid a hand on his arm. "Why would they send you checks?"

"Retirement pay for military service."

Her eyes widened in shock and there was no mistaking the victorious slant to his smile. "When were you in the service?"

"Up until last year."

Her thoughts scrambled. One question overlapped the other in her head. *Retirement pay?* "How long were you in altogether?"

He saluted her and grinned. "Twenty years, ma'am. United States Army."

She swallowed. She didn't know this man at all. "Twenty years," she repeated weakly. "That's a long time. Were you, uh, did you..." She didn't know quite how to ask this without possibly offending him. Sighing, she gave up on tact and asked, "What rank did you make it to?"

"Captain."

She shook her head in stunned disbelief. "Captain."

The pride in his eyes dimmed. "Why?"

"You had to be a kid when you joined."

"I was. I'd just turned seventeen. Even though I'd been in this country for two years by then, I had just gotten my green card."

"But you weren't a citizen yet? How did they let you join?"

"It's allowed, as long as you have a green card." He shrugged, the gesture nonchalant, but pride gleamed in his eyes again. "I figured the best way to show I deserved to be a citizen was to fight for my new country."

It seemed she couldn't stop shaking her head, to clear the fog, if nothing else. "That's why Dusty calls you Cap. It's not short for Cappel," she said, her mind spinning with small details.

John chuckled. "The kid isn't a bad helper, but he made a lousy soldier. He couldn't seem to get the discipline part down right."

Discipline. Routine. Rules. Boot camp. That was not a carefree life-style. She felt raw suddenly, devoid of the comfort of everything familiar. Like she'd been stripped and left out in the blistering sun with no defenses.

"What about your parents?" she asked calmly. "You were what, only fifteen when you got to America?"

He studied her closely for a silent moment before he answered. "My mother died before I started school. My father passed away the year before I left England. That's why I had to come over as an illegal alien." He looked down at her hand and brushed the back of his fingers across it. "I'm not proud of sneaking into the country that way, but it was either that or go into the equivalent of your foster care system."

He stared off and smiled as if recalling a fond memory. "I had one good year with a host family. That's where I learned carpentry."

"Why didn't you stay?"

"Mr. Sedworth died. They said it was a heart attack. They had six kids of their own. And Mrs. Sedworth sure didn't need another mouth to feed." He returned his gaze to her, his expression softening as he brought a hand to her cheek. "Hey, I didn't mean to make you sad. I've had a good life. No complaints from me."

Yes, her heart ached for the lonely, frightened fifteen-year-old he must have been, but she was annoyed, too. Or maybe she was just confused. "Why did you keep all this a secret?"

"It's not a secret." He frowned. "It just never came up in conversation. I'm proud of having served *my* country. I've been a citizen for over fifteen years, by the way."

"Yet you let me think you were some irresponsible drifter." She bit her lip. That was too strong an accusation, and not accurate. But she felt hurt, and betrayed somehow.

"I let you? You'd better think on that one again." His tone sharpened and his expression held an edgy hardness she hadn't seen before. "You chose to believe that about me. If you're referring to your house, I honored my contract." His jaw tightened, and he stared at the road ahead. "You want to talk about irresponsible? What do you call jumping to conclusions?"

That remark stung, but not half as much as the reality that John Cappel was not who she thought he was. Fifteen minutes ago, they'd had a safe relationship. Now they didn't. She pressed two fingers to her temple. Her head throbbed with all the confusing signals being broadcast from her brain.

Of course they still had a safe relationship. Safe for him, anyway. She loved him, and he'd promised her nothing. And she had readily accepted that. Except at the time, she'd thought he had nothing to promise her.

God, was she really this shallow a person? Because she now knew he had a respectable reputation, a steady paycheck, she suddenly felt differently toward him?

She let her head fall back against the seat. When she'd thought of John as a free spirit, a drifter who lived from job to job, she could put him in a nice little cubbyhole, one she fully understood. It was easy to accept the lack of ambition or discipline. Those qualities fit nicely into the cubbyhole, too.

But they no longer applied. He'd been a captain in the army, for goodness' sake. How much more driven and focused and disciplined could one get?

A horn honked, and she jumped. Tommie Nell waved as she drove past them in Jimmy's light blue pickup. Kelly sighed, and glanced over at John. He looked grim.

Her questions would definitely have to wait. He was edgy, probably rightfully so. And she had Gary to deal with yet, a chore she wasn't looking forward to, especially with so little sleep and scrambled eggs for brains.

And of course, now Tommie Nell had seen them sitting, inexplicably, on the side of the road, early, heading into town.

Kelly sighed again. "We'd better go," she said. "I think we've done enough damage for one day."

ENOUGH DAMAGE FOR ONE DAY?

Every time John replayed her last words in his head, he got good and royally ticked all over again. Is that what she thought of their lovemaking yesterday?

He swore under his breath as he filled another duffel bag. Bad enough she hadn't been impressed with his military service. Most women were. If not with his rank, at least with the uniform.

Bloody hell. He had a good mind to get it out of storage. He'd bet the rest of the women in Bachelor Falls wouldn't react so blandly, he thought, kicking aside an oak footstool he'd been carving.

Damn. It wasn't that he'd been trying to impress her, but that wasn't the point. She'd suddenly acted as though she couldn't wait to get rid of him.

He stopped in the middle of the cabin to look around at the mess he'd made while trying to pack. He didn't plan on leaving town immediately; he had some loose ends to tie up with Gary and the house and another side job. But packing what he didn't need for the next week before he finally did make his exit was good therapy.

Just the thought of leaving and never seeing Kelly again dealt a blow to his heart so acute that he gave the footstool an extra wallop just to relieve the pressure building in his chest.

He'd left women plenty of times before; that was part of a transient military life. That was one of the reasons he'd never gotten serious with any of them. But each time he made sure they knew the score before getting involved in any way. And each time it had still stung to leave. But nothing compared to the pain of just thinking about leaving Kelly.

Yet what choice did he have? She didn't want him. Oh, yeah, maybe for another couple of hours. He rearranged the two packed duffels with vicious precision. How had she put it? He wasn't the root of her problem and definitely not the solution. He'd thought about her odd comment often in the past two days, and he figured he knew what she meant.

He wasn't in the running. Not as a partner she

could love and respect. Kelly had very specific ideas about what she wanted in a marriage, in a husband. She wanted the house with the white picket fence and a man who was an accountant. Hell. He would never be a damn pencil pusher. That's why he'd finally retired. Because that's what the job was turning into.

He stretched his neck to the side to relieve the tension knotting the muscles there. Who knew what else went on in her head? He didn't. She hadn't bothered calling since he'd dropped her off yesterday. All he did know was that the longer he stuck around, the pricklier things could be for her. He had a feeling the good folks of Bachelor Falls had tongues that wagged more than forgave.

As much as it tore at him, the kindest thing he could do for her was to leave. And he would, by the end of the week, or sooner if he had the guts....

A knock at the door had his heart tripping over in his chest, his feet stumbling over the footstool. Maybe it was Kelly. Maybe he'd blown everything out of proportion in his head. Maybe they...

John swung open the door and stared at the short older woman in the red poodle skirt. He squinted trying to recall where he'd seen her before.

"Well, since you obviously don't know who I am, I'll tell you," she said with an impatient shake of her head. "At my age I can't wait around and play guessing games. I'm Ona Mae Hunyacre. Are you gonna ask me in?"

John pushed a weary hand through his hair. "Ah, Mrs. Hunyacre, the place is a mess and I, uh——"

"It's Miss Hunyacre, as if everyone doesn't know that from here to Branson." An odd smile lifted one side of her bright red lips when she mentioned Branson, and he frowned. Surely Kelly hadn't... "Well," she said, "it's mighty warm out here."

"Miss Hunyacre, I know why you're here and I can assure you there are no aliens hiding in my cabin."

"I don't know about that," she said, giving him the once-over. "Some guy wrote a book about men being from Mars, and I tend to agree." She pushed past him, grabbing ahold of his shirt as she strode by, and hauling him inside with her. "Listen, sonny, you and me are going to have a talk. And I don't care of it's in English, Martian or Bostian."

Chapter Seventeen

Kelly addressed the final un-invitation to her un-wedding, pushed the stack of envelopes to the side, folded her arms on the kitchen table and laid the side of her head on her crossed wrists. Everything she'd done had taken such a huge effort this past week, sucking the life and energy right out of her until she was too drained to think about anything but brushing her teeth and crawling into bed.

And it had all been her own doing. As soon as she'd explained her feelings to Gary, she knew with crystal clarity that she'd been pushing the poor man too hard for too long. The relief that had sprung to his expression when she admitted she no longer wanted to get married would have been laughable had it been part of a cartoon. But this was real life and she'd done a good job of screwing things up for both him and herself. Fortunately, he didn't blame her. But she'd known he wouldn't. That wasn't his way. She was lucky he still called her his friend.

Too bad John didn't.

She sniffed, thinking about the times she'd been tempted to pick up the phone, then talked herself out of it. Some of that had been stubbornness on her part, the rest was pride. He simply didn't want her like she wanted him. Love and chemistry appeared to be two different issues.

Men. They all need to be shipped to...to Bost.

"Yoo-hoo."

Kelly straightened, bringing up her head and dabbing at her eyes when she heard Ona Mae's voice at the back door.

Her friend didn't wait for an invitation, but instead opened the screen door and stepped into the kitchen. She squinted at Kelly. "How far do you think that sniffling is going to get you?"

"Not now, Ona Mae." Didn't this woman have a home anymore? She'd been bugging Kelly for three days in a row now, telling her more than she wanted to know. She'd already heard that John was leaving next week. That pretty much summed up everything she needed to know. "I mean it," Kelly added.

The older woman chuckled. "I'm glad you're beginning to sound like your old self."

Wrong. Kelly wasn't ever going to be her old self. Never again. Not after having made love with John. A piece of her would always be with him, no matter where he went.

She, at least, would have the satisfaction of knowing she hadn't settled for something less than love. Great consolation.

Ona Mae pulled out a chair, and Kelly sighed with resignation, and asked, "Did you at least bring chocolate?"

"I'm too depressed to think about chocolate. Besides, I know you haven't been eating anyway."

"You're depressed?" Kelly straightened. She'd never her that admission before. "What's wrong?"

"I've been thinking a lot about Lowell lately."

Kelly made a disgusted face. "Nice try." She knew what the woman was up to. Kelly had made the mistake of telling her a little about John, not everything, but enough for Ona Mae to get a picture. "You're going to tell me how my moping has got you thinking about how your ex-fiancé got abducted by aliens, and then you'll try to manipulate—"

Briskly shaking her head, Ona Mae cut her off. "Oh, no, you have nothing to do with it." She sighed dramatically. "Although I suppose John's leaving today is partly responsible for all these dreadful—"

"Today?" Kelly practically shrieked. "He's leaving *today?*"

Her friend nodded, as if that fact was of no real concern. As if the world hadn't just tipped sideways. "He's all packed up, his car stuffed to the brim." Ona Mae sniffed. "Just like the day my Lowell left."

Kelly had sprung from her chair and started pacing the small kitchen. Until a moment ago, she realized she'd still had hope, hope that he'd call, hope that he'd tell her he couldn't live without her. But instead he was leaving. And without saying goodbye.

Her heart constricted with a painful twist, and she stopped in the middle of a stride to catch her breath. Staring into Ona Mae's forlorn face, something registered in Kelly's brain.

"What do you mean Lowell was packed up the day he left? I thought he was abducted by aliens."

"Oh, that." Ona Mae waved a hand. "You didn't expect me to admit to these busybodies around here that he left me, did you?'' She shook her head, and Kelly knew the sadness in the older woman's eyes was genuine. ''That's not to say I don't know there aren't aliens out there,'' she added quickly. Then her features settled into sorrow again. ''To be fair, Lowell didn't exactly leave me. I just didn't have the guts to go with him. And I've regretted it every day of my life.''

''So he did leave you.''

''No, he left Bachelor Falls. And I couldn't.''

Kelly stared at the woman who'd been a friend, a mother, a grandmother all rolled into one dependable sounding board. And all she could see was John's face when she'd brushed aside his attempt to tell her of his accomplishments. His pride had been hurt. She recognized the signs. If it hadn't been for Ona Mae, there would have been many times Kelly would've had no one to tell about the *A* she'd gotten in math, or that she'd made the honor roll.

Kelly smiled to herself. If Ona Mae really was manipulating her, she was doing a terrific job because Kelly made up her mind right then and there to stop John. If only to tell him how she felt. The rest would be up to him.

''I have to run. Let yourself out, okay?'' Kelly grabbed her keys off the counter, then stooped to kiss Ona Mae's cheek.

''Don't worry about me,'' Ona Mae said, smiling, and no longer looking the least bit sad.

Kelly slid her a suspicious look, and laughed. ''I wouldn't dream of it.''

When she pushed open the screen door, she saw John's black Jeep parked off to the left. Out of the corner of her eye, she saw him heading for the front door. Her heart slammed against her chest.

Maybe he sensed her presence, or maybe her heart had really slammed that hard and he heard it, but he stopped right before he was about to step up on the porch, and turned toward her.

"Hi." She gave him a small wave, a sudden attack of nerves making her feel as shy as a newborn kitten.

He half smiled and changed direction. His gaze drew to the keys that she was clutching so tightly in her hand she thought she might break something. "I'm catching you at a bad time," he said.

"Oh, no," she said quickly, "I was just, uh… No, this isn't a bad time."

"Good." He pushed a hand through his hair. "So, how have you been?"

"Busy." She moistened her parched lips. "And you?"

"Yeah." His gaze fastened on her mouth for a second or two, then he blew out a breath and glanced distractedly at the hedge under her kitchen window. "You're going to need to prune that soon." He shrugged. "If you want I could probably do that for you on Saturday."

"I know it's growing like—" She stopped. "On Saturday? I thought you were leaving…"

The screen door squeaked open behind her.

John looked over her shoulder, and smiled. "Good morning, Miss Hunyacre."

Kelly slowly turned and narrowed her eyes. "Ona Mae?"

"Did I say today?" Shaking her head, her *former* friend averted her cagey hazel eyes as she sprinted down the steps and walked past them toward the driveway. "You know, my mind just isn't what it used to be."

"Right," Kelly said, and John frowned at her tone.

"Seems I did come at a bad time," he said.

Kelly inhaled deeply. "Actually, I was on my way to see you."

"You were?" His expression remained disconcertingly blank.

It gave her a brief pause, but didn't stop her. She took another quick breath. "I wanted to see how you were...and to tell you that I, uh...that I was wondering where you were headed next," she finished lamely as self-disappointment filled every pore in her body.

She had to tell him she loved him no matter how he took the news. And that she was willing to go with him if he'd have her. Living in Bachelor Falls imprisoned by regret no longer appealed to her.

"Funny you should mention that," he said, then visibly swallowed. "I heard there's this new house for sale. It's not quite finished yet, but hey, as luck would have it, I'm a carpenter."

Her pulse picked up speed. "Oh. Is it around here?"

"Real close."

"I see."

"It's big though. Too big for one person." He moved a shoulder. "Probably a good size for a family."

"Oh."

"One problem."

"Huh?" The word came out a croak. Her voice

was no longer working, because his expression was no longer blank. Tenderness and uncertainty colored the anxious eyes roaming her face in inquiry.

"I'm not sure the lady I have in mind to share the house with wants to marry me."

The air fled Kelly's lungs. She tried to inhale but it was a useless effort, one that merely earned her a burning sensation in her chest.

"Have you told her how you feel? I mean I assume you l-love her."

"I do. But I've been too busy being a jackass and nursing my ego to tell her."

A smile twitched at the corners of Kelly's mouth no matter how hard she tried to stop it. "I thought you wanted to finish seeing the world."

"I did, or I thought I did." His lips curved, too. "Then this lady showed up in my life and screwed up all my plans."

She sobered. "I'll go with you."

Shaking his head, he reached out a hand and cupped her jaw. "No. Our kids will need roots. I don't want any military brats," he said. "I've seen more than my share of what a transient life does to kids. Besides, Bachelor Falls is a nice place. Look how well you grew up."

Kids? He wanted children. Their children. Her breath caught again. Her emotions were already a mess. She didn't know if she could take all this without bawling like a baby herself. "But I don't want you to look back and—"

"Shhh." He brushed his thumb across her lips. "The only regret I could possibly have is if I walked away from you. I love you, Kelly. More than I thought possible.''

"I love you," she whispered, and pressed her cheek into his warm palm. "That's what I was coming to tell you."

He smiled, briefly closed his eyes and hugged her to him. "I'm not going to be an accountant or an office jockey, though. Will that disappoint you?"

"Of course not." She tried to pull back to look at him, to make sure he understood that she would never try to tell him what to do, that she was proud of him just the way he was. But he kept her close.

"I make a good living at carpentry, and I figure I'll start keeping most of my retirement check." He paused. "Remember I told you about the Sedworths, the family who took care of me back in England?" She nodded without moving her head from his chest. "I've been sending her money every month, but the kids are all out of college now, and she's been begging me to stop for the past three years. When she finds out I'm getting married—"

This time she did pull back to stare at him. "Have you sent her money all these years?"

"Yeah." He lifted a shoulder, looking uncomfortable. "But like I said, now that I'll have my own family, that'll stop."

She threw her arms around him and nearly knocked him over. "You will not stop. Not on my account, anyway. You are a wonderful, wonderful man who I fall more and more in love with every time I find out something new about you."

"Hey." He started laughing as he tried to maintain his balance and keep them both upright.

"Despite what you think about all my freebie services, I make a pretty good living myself. Our kids will be very well cared for, and they are going to have everything they need, including two parents who adore each other, who love them beyond reason and who very much care what they bring home in their report cards each quarter."

She stopped long enough to take a breath and noticed how stern his face had become. Her heart thudded with dread. "What's the matter?"

His frowned deepened. "You're damn right we'll care about their report cards, I expect—"

"Oh, boy, you're going to be one of those." She started laughing, then pressed her lips to his before he could say another word.

His abrupt smile tempered the kiss, and when she reared back to smile, too, he said, "And after they bring home their perfect report cards, their mama is going to teach them how to paint pretty pictures."

Her grin faded. "Why would—" She blinked. "You know? How?" She felt strange, exposed. "It's just a flaky hobby."

"It is not. It's a talent. One you should be very proud of."

His face and voice were both adamant, and she felt the smile return to her lips. Actually, she didn't have much talent at all, but she did have fun painting. She didn't know how he knew her little secret, and she didn't care.

As long as he always looked at her the way he was looking at her now, with the smile on his lips reaching his eyes, turning them the color of promise. A promise that he was going to be there for her every day in every possible way.

The kind of promise that made her glow. *Just like Lana and Ellie,* she thought as she lifted her lips to his.

He kissed her gently at first, and then their kiss grew hungry and urgent.

Somewhere in the distance, someone sighed. Then it turned to a cough.

Ona Mae. Kelly had almost forgotten about her friend. Kelly broke the kiss and turned to look over her shoulder.

Ona Mae was poking into the basket of her bicycle.

"Well, well," she said, "look who finally decided to turn up." Reaching into the battered white wicker, she pulled out Purple Bunny and grinned at Kelly. "Looks like the little rascal brought you luck, after all."

The bunny's ear was limper than cooked squash and one eye was still missing, but darned if he didn't look like he was smiling.

Kelly's eyes narrowed even while a grin tugged stubbornly at her lips. "Ona Mae."

Ona Mae narrowed her eyes right back, and scrunched her mouth up. "It was the Bostians who had him." Her hand suddenly jerked up to shade her eyes and, tilting her head back, she peered at the clear blue sky. "Did you see it? Did you? That was their spaceship, all right." She continued to watch for a moment longer, then made a huffing sound and hopped on her bike and started pedaling away. "Bold little devils—they usually wait till nightfall."

Kelly couldn't hold back her laughter any longer.

She looked at John's stricken face, and asked, "You still want to stay?"

His brows drawing thoughtfully together, he rubbed his jaw. "What did you think of Branson?"

**Head Down Under for twelve tales of heated
romance in beautiful and untamed Australia!**

**Here's a sneak preview of the first novel in
THE AUSTRALIANS**

Outback Heat by Emma Darcy
available July 1998

'HAVE I DONE something wrong?' Angie persisted, wishing Taylor would emit a sense of camaraderie instead of holding an impenetrable reserve.

'Not at all,' he assured her. 'I would say a lot of things right. You seem to be fitting into our little Outback community very well. I've heard only good things about you.'

'They're nice people,' she said sincerely. Only the Maguire family kept her shut out of their hearts.

'Yes,' he agreed. 'Though I appreciate it's taken considerable effort from you. It is a world away from what you're used to.'

The control Angie had been exerting over her feelings snapped. He wasn't as blatant as his aunt in his prejudice against her but she'd felt it coming through every word he'd spoken and she didn't deserve any of it.

'Don't judge me by your wife!'

His jaw jerked. A flicker of some dark emotion destroyed the steady power of his probing gaze.

'No two people are the same. If you don't know that, you're a man of very limited vision. So I come from the city as your wife did! That doesn't stop me from being an individual in my own right.'

She straightened up, proudly defiant, furiously angry with the situation. 'I'm *me*. Angie Cordell. And it's time you took the blinkers off your eyes, Taylor Maguire.'

Then she whirled away from him, too agitated by the explosive expulsion of her emotion to keep facing him.

The storm outside hadn't yet eased. There was nowhere to go. She stopped at the window, staring blindly at the torrential rain. The thundering on the roof was almost deafening but it wasn't as loud as the silence behind her.

'You want me to go, don't you? You've given me a month's respite and now you want me to leave and channel my energies somewhere else.'

'I didn't say that, Angie.'

'You were working your way around it.' Bitterness at his tactics spewed the suspicion. 'Do you have your first choice of governess waiting in the wings?'

'No. I said I'd give you a chance.'

'Have you?' She swung around to face him. 'Have you really, Taylor?'

He hadn't moved. He didn't move now except to make a gesture of appeasement. 'Angie, I was merely trying to ascertain how you felt.'

'Then let me tell you your cynicism was shining through every word.'

He frowned, shook his head. 'I didn't mean to hurt you.' The blue eyes fastened on hers with devastating sincerity. 'I truly did not come in here to take you down or suggest you leave.'

Her heart jiggled painfully. He might be speaking the truth but the judgements were still there, the judgements that ruled his attitude towards her, that kept her shut out of his life, denied any real sharing with him, denied his confidence and trust. She didn't know why it meant so much to her but it did. It did. And the need to fight for justice from him was as much a raging torrent inside her as the rain outside.

The spring 1998 forecast calls for...

Showers

April 1998: **HERE COMES THE...BABY**
Pam McCutcheon

A front of morning sickness sets in with temperatures rising at the onset of a sexy secret dad. Highs: Too hot!

May 1998: **A BACHELOR FALLS**
Karen Toller Whittenburg

Heavy gusts of romance continue as a warming trend turns friends to lovers just in time for one friend's wedding...to someone else!

June 1998: **BRIDE TO BE...OR NOT TO BE?** Debbi Rawlins

Expect a heat wave as the handsome hunk building a bride's dream house sends soaring temperatures through her fantasies.

Available wherever Harlequin books are sold.

Take 2 bestselling love stories FREE

Plus get a FREE surprise gift!

Special Limited-Time Offer

Mail to Harlequin Reader Service®

3010 Walden Avenue
P.O. Box 1867
Buffalo, N.Y. 14240-1867

YES! Please send me 2 free Harlequin American Romance® novels and my free surprise gift. Then send me 4 brand-new novels every month, which I will receive months before they appear in bookstores. Bill me at the low price of $3.34 each plus 25¢ delivery and applicable sales tax, if any.* That's the complete price, and a saving of over 10% off the cover prices—quite a bargain! I understand that accepting the books and gift places me under no obligation ever to buy any books. I can always return a shipment and cancel at any time. Even if I never buy another book from Harlequin, the 2 free books and the surprise gift are mine to keep forever.

154 HEN CH7E

Name	(PLEASE PRINT)	
Address	Apt. No.	
City	State	Zip

This offer is limited to one order per household and not valid to present Harlequin American Romance® subscribers. *Terms and prices are subject to change without notice. Sales tax applicable in N.Y.

Presents Extravaganza

25 YEARS!

It's our birthday and we're celebrating....

Twenty-five years of romance fiction
featuring men of the world and captivating women—
Seduction and passion guaranteed!

Not only are we promising you three months of terrific
books, authors and romance, but as an added **bonus**
with the retail purchase of two Presents® titles,
you can receive a special one-of-a-kind keepsake.
It's our gift to you!

Look in the back pages of any Harlequin Presents® title,
from May to July 1998, for more details.

Available wherever Harlequin books are sold.

HARLEQUIN®

DEBBIE MACOMBER

invites you to the

HEART OF TEXAS

Join Debbie Macomber as she brings you the lives
and loves of the folks in the ranching community
of Promise, Texas.

If you loved Midnight Sons—don't miss
Heart of Texas! A brand-new six-book series
from Debbie Macomber.

Available in February 1998
at your favorite retail store.

Heart of Texas by Debbie Macomber

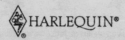

HARLEQUIN®

HPHRT1